LEXI GREENE

Shatterproof

First published by Warrior Heart Publishing 2019

This novel is entirely a work of fiction. The names, characters and incidents portrayed in it are the work of the author's imagination. Any resemblance to actual persons, living or dead, events or localities is entirely coincidental.

First edition

ISBN: 978-0-6483874-6-6

This book was professionally typeset on Reedsy.
Find out more at reedsy.com

To the Glass Children

Foreword

Emily Stone, an internationally successful model on the brink of supermodel stardom, appears to have it all. All, except love, because Emily wants the kind of man who isn't fooled by the pretty. She wants the kind of love that's big enough and true enough to include her disabled sister and dysfunctional mother.

Nick was an A-list actor in tinsel town with a super-sized ego until a tragic car accident stole his wife, his unborn child, and his gilded career, leaving him physically and emotionally scarred.

When wintry French Island brings these two wayward souls home, shared childhood memories aren't enough to bridge the deep divide forged by their adult lives and choices.

That is until Carmie, Emily's delightful Down Syndrome sister, weaves her special kind of magic. Can Carmie's boundless love and infectious joy help them to heal their broken hearts or will the glamour of Emily's work-world whisk her away?

Acknowledgement

A big thank you to my writing community, and to the women from RWAusralia and RWAmerica who inspire and support me including Beverley Eikli, Nina Campbell, Joanne Dannon, Melanie Milburne, and Margie Lawson... thank you. And a huge thanks to my brilliant editor, Jena O'Connor, my proof-reader, Janice Owen, and my talented cover artist, Charmaine Ross!

Prologue

Emily Stone wriggled her toes in the smooth, silky soft, pure silica sand of Whitehaven Beach, and let the gossamer thin wrap fall from her shoulder exposing the leopard print strap of the latest Mimale Animale string bikini. She angled her head towards the camera and the man behind it—Phillip Campbell—photographer extraordinaire from *Glamour Magazine*. A coveted jewel in her warrior crown—*Vogue, Elle, Harper's Bazaar, W Magazine, Glamour*—and a vital stepping-stone towards the dais of Victoria's Secret Angel. Phillip was about a decade older than her twenty-five years and when the camera lowered, his eyes burned with I-want-you-more-than-my-next-breath. His gaze feathered her flesh and her skin prickled, her heart ever so slightly skittish. Not the good kind of skittish. The kind that shifted in her stomach like an oyster left too long in the Queensland sun.

When had their friendship crossed the line towards something more serious?

She didn't do serious and now she would have to tell him, and in her experience that never went well. Men liked to think they were irresistible, and men with an ego like Phillip's? She'd probably lose the cover and worse, the friendship she'd come to value.

But this was theatre and she was the leading lady. She loaded the kind of smile that left a man weak and wanting and softened her gaze with erotic invitation. Phillip went rigid like she'd speared him somewhere vital and her inner warrior rejoiced.

The ultra-skimpy fabric covered her main bits—barely—and her gaze lowered to the golden globe of her shoulder. The click of the camera was machine-gun rapid, and Phillip prowled around her like a panther, his limbs bare, his body outstretched to capture an angle.

She kneeled in the sand, her left hip pushed to the side. The high cut bikini—known officially as a sky-scraper bottom—flattered and drew the eye to her waist. A guy with a big fan created enough wind to push her hair back from her face and cool her skin. It was warm. Hot even. And the sky stretched blue and vast above. There was the call of a gull, the chatter of birds in the scrub that lined the beach. The air was tangy with salt, but there was a sweet undertone from the native flowers that bloomed beneath the canopy of trees. This section of the Whitsunday Island beach was distant from the yachts and the tourists, who sought the pristine wilderness of one of the world's most unspoiled and beautiful beaches—thank goodness. She liked the eye of the camera, but she had no taste for spectators.

"Let's head into the water. I want you wet." Phillip's tone was gravelly, like the one hundred percent pure silica sand had lodged in his throat.

Emily didn't miss the sexual innuendo, but she chose to ignore it. "If this bikini gets wet, it will cling even closer than it does already."

"It certainly will." His smile seared her skin. "It's yours to keep, sweetie. No harm done."

Like she could wear this anywhere except in a photo shoot. The cut was too daring and the ripe pomegranate colour near dripped with sexual invitation.

Phillip backed into the water, his tanned legs bare, his chest bare, his face hidden by the camera. He was a virulent man. A man in his prime. A predator in the industry.

Emily sauntered into the crystal-clear water of the Great Barrier Reef, her friend-turned-foe circling her like a shark in the water. Click. Click. The water was cool after what seemed like hours on the boat and the beach.

"Dive in. Curve your very toned butt through the air." His voice sounded breathless like she was his very own sexual fantasy.

She did as she was told and dived deep into the arms of the sea, before bursting back into the light. She rose like a sea-goddess, a shower of crystal-like drops catching the sun. She heard a volley of clicks, punctuated by a groan. She loved her job. How could she not? She let her head fall back, her hair a silky wet curtain, her face tipped to the sun.

"You're killing me, honey. Don't move."

She smiled like her back didn't ache and did as she was told like she was biddable or witless or fooled by his adoration. She hoped like hell this photo shoot would see her on the cover of *Glamour Magazine*, but there was a very fine line between stroking a man's ego and compromising her own integrity. She needed to go home. She needed to regroup. She needed to remind herself why she worked so hard.

"Here. Put these on." Sunglasses of one designer brand or another were thrust into her hand and she gratefully lowered them onto her face. Click. Click. Click.

"Okay, sweetheart. I want you to walk out of the water like you're a mermaid princess who's ditched her tail and grown legs, her eyes on a prince."

That took some conjuring, but she pulled it off. Her body was a weapon, her face, ammunition. Phillip appeared enraptured, which in this industry was good… and bad.

"That was perfect." He came up beside her and when his arm brushed against hers, her skin puckered like a cold breeze had come off the water. He was a man used to getting what he wanted, but what he wanted was something she couldn't give. He'd fallen for the illusion, which had as much substance as his elongated shadow.

"What did you think of the shots?" She strove to keep her tone nonchalant, like his opinion didn't have the cut and thrust of a guillotine. He could sniff out weakness like a well-trained hound.

"They're good. Really good."

"Good enough for the cover?" Her skin crawled with fire-ants. She didn't want him to know how important this was to her.

"We'll see. I can't make any promises." There was a predatory gleam in his eyes.

"Of course." She stepped towards the esky and reached for two bottles of water. She felt his eyes on her, knowing every move was watched, and revered, and worshipped. It infused her with invincible strength and lifted her from ordinary and cursed to fairytale queen.

The uber-expensive, celebrity-favoured Qualia resort on Hamilton Island in the Whitsundays was one of Emily's favourite places. No longer behind the camera, but across the dinner table at the Long Pavilion, Phillip's gaze adored. His eyes feasted.

Emily took a sip of her wine and eyed Phillip over the rim of the glass. He was fabulously good looking, and confidence oozed from every pore. She'd risk her career if she got too close—and she'd risk her career if she didn't.

"This is our fifth unofficial date." He took her free hand in his and stroked her palm.

Even as their eyes connected and her heart stirred—what woman didn't like to be adored? —she knew this had to stop. Flirting was fun until it wasn't.

"Five dates and counting." He smiled and his cheeks puckered into well-worn creases, his skin tanned and leathery.

Five dates and over. She'd miss his friendship. She'd miss the woman she was through his eyes. Like she was more, rather than less.

The sun hung low and heavy in the sky, and the coral sea stretched before them, a sparkling, pink-tinged extravaganza. The air was warm with a barely-there breeze. She soaked in the sounds of the music and the night—the scents of the earth and the sea. She basked in his attention, in his selfish adoration. They'd devoured an exquisite share-platter of local reef fish, Whitsunday bugs, grilled prawns, sautéed cuttlefish, and scallops. Emily took the second to last truffle fry and gazed across the lush vegetation to the sea. The sun slipped softly, quietly, slowly over the horizon and a barrage of insects called and fussed, heralding in the night.

He could give her everything she wanted.

No. He couldn't.

"Thank you for the lovely dinner. I love it here. It's so beautiful." The candle flickered and danced.

"You are so beautiful."

The circular stroke of his thumb against her palm ebbed and flowed like the waves below, whispering all kinds of promises that left her heated and wanting and hopeful and stupid.

Her gaze lowered to the glint of the diamond on the fourth finger of her right hand. Her best friend, Charliese's ring. Her touchstone for the past two years. *I want you to have this. Wear it as a warning. Be careful with your heart...* Charliese had been disillusioned about love and marriage, and pregnant by a man she'd seen behind her husband's back. It wasn't like Emily needed the warning, but she wore it because Charliese's friendship had been important to her.

She tightened her invisible armour around her.

She had a five-date rule for a reason. To protect her heart. To protect her family who relied on her for everything. What shone in Phillip's eyes wasn't the kind of love she wanted—the kind her grandparents had shared. What razed there wasn't real.

Phillip was a man used to getting what he wanted and what he wanted was to get into her panties. He didn't love her. He couldn't. He was in love with a fantasy. This was about stroking his ego.

Fire was fun until it burned.

Emily's phone buzzed and she glanced down. *You need to get your skinny arse back here asap. Your mother and sister need you. You may not care, but I do. Nick*

Her brow clenched. Her heart thudded. Her thoughts scattered like she'd been hit by a grenade. Nick Wheatley? She reached for her water and gulped it down. Her mother and sister had been fine when she'd gone home two months ago. Besides she paid Julia McKenzie a ridiculous amount of money to take care of them.

Phillip's gaze locked on hers—grey and stormy, seductive and steady. "Bad news?"

Her chest tightened. "I need to go home. First thing tomorrow."

"Is someone dying?"

"No, I don't think so."

"Then I'll book you a flight myself—at the end of the day. The last flight. Not the first. You're a professional. You need to finish the shoot. We've hired a yacht for tomorrow."

Emily's thoughts whirled. He was right. She couldn't just pack up her itsy-bitsy bikini and leave. There were a whole lot of people relying on her. This was business. *Big* business. This was how she paid the bills. "I need to call home." She got to her feet and strode towards the front of the restaurant, seeking privacy.

No answer. Her heart pitched and rolled in her chest. Why wasn't her mum answering? She punched more digits.

"Hello?"

"Julia, what's going on? I just received a text from Nick Wheatley saying mum and Carmie are in a terrible state." Her breath was short and quick, like she'd run to the top of One Tree Hill. She pushed through the door and out into the leafy entry, unable to stand still.

"I wouldn't know. Your mother fired me about four weeks ago. I'm still waiting for my severance pay."

"Why didn't you tell me? There's nobody looking after them?" She fought to slow her breath, to calm the crazy thud of her heart, to gulp the warm night air.

"She told me if I spoke to you, I'd lose my entitlements, which she hasn't paid anyway. Did she tell you she was diagnosed with Chronic Fatigue Syndrome?"

"I spoke with her yesterday and no, she didn't mention it." Chronic Fatigue? That could take months if not years to recover from. How could Julia have just left them? "My mother needs you. *I* need you."

"There's no way I'm going back and if I'm not paid my entitlements—by tomorrow—I'm taking legal action."

Emily shivered like Melbourne's wintry chill had migrated north and permeated her bones. "I'll arrange payment tonight." The adrenaline that had forced her to pace drained away and she plonked down onto a low stone wall.

"Good luck getting someone else to take the job."

Emily hung up and her dinner shifted uncomfortably in her stomach. It was like her soul was pierced by a hook and whenever she got too comfortable in her own skin, she was reeled back. Back to the rural island in Western Port Bay off mainland Melbourne where she grew up before her time. Back to being less than she wanted to be. Back to being in close proximity to Nick Wheatley, which stung like a thousand lashes. The sweet scent of the frangipani and hibiscus seemed to wrap around her throat, cloying and suffocating.

"Are you okay?"

Her two worlds collided. Phillip. The shoot. The magazine. Air found its way in. The dizzy sensation cleared. "Yes, I'm fine. Thank you."

"I've booked you a late-afternoon flight tomorrow. We'll need to make an early start in the morning, so I've changed your wake-up call to five. I've let the rest of the crew know."

"Thank you. That's very kind."

"Your happiness is important to me."

Emily felt a shift in the air around her. Like it had thickened and pressed too close. Her hair follicles tightened. Her vision darkened. "I need some water."

Phillip wrapped his arm around her and led her back to their table. She sank into her chair and reached for her glass. The sea below was black and churning. The island across the strait loomed like a monster about to pounce.

"What happened?"

"The woman who looks after my mum and sister, and manages our B&B walked out about a month ago. I need to go home and sort things out."

"I like you, Emily. I like that you care about your family. I like that you treat others with respect." Phillip's tone was like warm caramel. He reached out and took her hand. A different girl would be swept away. A different girl would be spellbound. A different girl would want everything the Dark Lord in his eyes promised.

"I like you, too, but…"

Twilight pressed around Emily like a gossamer veil. Crickets clacked in the undergrowth like a warning. She took a too-fast gulp of her wine, a pulse pounding in her ears, a pulse pounding between her thighs.

He smiled the kind of smile that left a girl weak and wanting. Emily pressed her palm against the rough invitation of his, their fingers interlacing. The contact stirred wishes and whispers in the warm night air.

Emily's heart snagged like a shard of glass in her chest.

"I need to say good-night. We have an early start." She pulled back and saw the flash of disappointment in his eyes. The burning desire.

"If you're sure that's what you want?"

"It is." She took a deep breath and steadied the erratic thud of her pulse. "I'm sorry, Phillip. I appreciate your friendship very much, but I'm not interested in a sexual relationship. With any man. I have other priorities right now." He deserved her honesty even if it cost her the front cover of *Glamour*.

Silence wrapped around her throat like a too-tight scarf caught in the wheel of a slow-moving convertible.

Kerthump. Kerthump. Why didn't he speak? Had any woman ever said no? Probably not. It was professional suicide.

"I'm sorry, too, my dear. Go home and sort out your problems, then come back to me and we'll work this out." He turned her hand over in his and lowered his lips to the inside of her palm. Her skin tingled from the soft touch and she fought the urge to snatch it back.

He hadn't heard her. He didn't want to hear her.

Emily rose to her feet, a frustrated scream behind her carefully arranged smile. "I'll see you in the morning."

"Sleep well, my dear."

Emily turned away and his gaze on her back was a searing flame.

Chapter One

Emily stood on the rear deck of the Western Port Ferry in the bone-chilling cold. Her skinny jeans and soft-as-a-kitten Italian leather boots weren't suited to the bitter elements, but she'd take the aggrieved gust of the wind and the cold cut of the air over the eyes of the small gaggle of people who huddled inside the cabin. She pulled her merino wrap tighter, but the winter-chill found its way in. The weather couldn't have been more different from the warmth of the Whitsunday Islands. Her gaze settled on the moon-like stretch of rocks and sand, the colour of despair. At half-tide, the shoreline at Stony Point had little appeal beyond the pelican that stood on an age-old post from a long-forgotten pier.

The engines let out a guttural roar and the green-grey sudsy water slapped against the side of the hull as the vessel gained momentum. Emily reached for the metal railing, thick with marine paint, rust pushing up from beneath like a festering boil. Her gaze shifted to the horizon, shrouded in mist. Somewhere behind it was a dark splotch of land—French Island.

Home.

Already she felt the warmth of it soothe her soul. A trip home was just what she needed to regroup and reset her priorities. Phillip's cool withdrawal had left her as melancholy as the

Melbourne winter. A rusted blade, long lodged in her heart, shifted and spliced, but she knew the drill. It was a pheromone thing. A physical phenomenon that would pass. She was better off alone. Stronger. Safer.

The ring on her right finger glittered like frost. Look where love had taken her best friend... into the dark, dank earth.

Emily gripped the handle of her suitcase like a time-traveller. Or a traveller between worlds—the fantasy world of make-up and hair-straighteners, bikinis and spray tans—and the small community of French Island. The island might be big, but it was mostly national park and farmland. The short twenty-minute ferry ride belied the enormity of her metamorphosis from glamorous international model to bullied and belittled younger sister of Carmen Stone (thank God those school-ground battles were behind her) and dutiful daughter of Beverley Stone.

Beverley, now better known by her maiden name, Beverley Straun, was an artist and owner of the Mosquito Creek Bed and Breakfast, a mud brick, gabled, self-contained country retreat on Mosquito Creek Road.

Emily squashed the twinge of guilt—it was more like a welt or a gash or an arterial bleed. And that rusted blade in her heart? It was anger, old but sharp. Anger at her lily-livered father who'd run out on them the moment the going got tough. Well, tough*er*. As a nine-year-old, she'd blamed Carmie, her nickname for Carmen, but the truth was lodged in Emily's heart like a blade in stone. He hadn't loved *her* enough to stay.

Emily's stomach heaved as the deck angled critically towards the green-grey sudsy swash of the bay and the motor's growl became a scream, a battle cry as it conquered the swell and surged onwards through waves, whipped and stirred by the wind. Every hard-won metre tightened the knot that throbbed inside her.

She couldn't stay for long. Not when a battalion of barracouta beauties snapped at her stilettos, wanting what she'd worked so hard to earn.

She needed a new manager for the B&B. One who could nurse her mum and ensure her sister was supervised and supported in the business, then she needed to get back to making a living and creating a buffer for their future. Modelling was a time-limited career and she needed to strike while her curling iron was hot.

The Tankerton Jetty loomed out of the mist, the low-lying cloud threatening drizzle. Her skin was tight from the briny sea air, and her ponytail was damp and tangled by the wind. Her gaze scanned the near-empty pier. There was no sign of her mum, which shouldn't have hurt.

A fisherman sat with his bucket and rod, dressed in yellow wet-weather gear, his attention on his line. She'd be surprised if fish were biting in this cauldron of hell.

"Not a day that shows off her best attributes."

Emily spun around and her heart did that rollercoaster thing where it stopped, suspended in no-motion before pitching downwards at dizzying speed. Her already chilled skin puckered and pinched, and the need for flight roared in her ears. Nick Wheatley. Charliese's would-have-been ex-husband… if she'd lived long enough to divorce him. He loomed in the doorway to the cabin, his hands gripping the marine-metal architrave.

Emily observed the ugly welt of a scar that slashed his right cheek, her eyes widening. Gone was the perfect symmetry that brought him Hollywood fame. Gone was the perfect blue of his razor-sharp eyes, lost in a snarl of violets and blacks. His right eye was swollen and shiny, his lip split like he'd been in a bar fight. His golden blond hair was dishevelled, and he reeked of alcohol. It seeped from his pores and his breath and his mussed hair. It seemed his life had taken a turn for the worse.

Good.

Emily's grip tightened on her wrap and she shifted her gaze to the rocky shore, dotted with mangroves. She took a deep breath of the fishy, salty, rancid air and faced the poor excuse for a man. His mother had died not six months before and she owed him for contacting her, so she fought to be civil. "Good morning."

His gaze dropped to her Louis Vuitton suitcase. "You got my message." His lip curled as he spoke, the scar tissue pulling tighter than the rest. She heard the unspoken censure, which was rich coming from him.

"Yes, thank you." It wasn't like she owed him an explanation. "I was sorry to hear about your mum." *About the car accident. About your wife.*

"Thanks." His stormy gaze moved towards the pitching horizon. "I haven't seen you in a while. Not since…" His hands dug deep into the pockets of his coat, his shoulders dragging forward like the baggage he carried outweighed the rocks in her suitcase.

"No." Not since before the accident. She hadn't wanted to see him. In fact, she'd actively avoided him. Her long-ago crush was dead and buried, along with her closest friend. He'd left the island to become a Hollywood star and she'd been young enough to be impressed by his liaisons and party-boy ways splashed through the magazines stocked at the general store. By the time he'd married Charliese, he'd been less of a man and more of an ego. "I've been busy with work, but I visit as often as I can."

"Short visits from what I've heard."

Emily didn't miss the bitterness or the judgement. "Big night?"

"I get out sometimes." His scowl deepened into well-worn tracts across his brow. His cheeks were dark with man-growth and he looked scruffy, like he didn't give a toss.

With his mother gone, why hadn't he packed his bags and scuttled back to LA at the first opportunity? Because his face was no longer Hollywood perfect, and his ego would never recover? She eyed the hand-knitted sweater and the breadth of his chest beneath the practical raincoat. He'd changed over the years. Not that Emily had known him well. He was older than her by a good seven years and he'd left the island in his teens to attend a private boarding school. Even married to her closest friend, their paths had rarely crossed. He'd seemed so worldly and glamorous. More in love with himself than his wife, it turned out. More in love with the booze and the Hollywood parties. No wonder Charliese had felt lonely and ignored. No wonder she'd been drawn to the father of her child, a man who couldn't bring her happiness, not while she wore Nick's ring.

Charliese's death had been convenient for Nick. He hadn't had to face a messy divorce or the fall-out from his wife's pregnancy. He'd received sympathy when he deserved animosity. The thought brought a wintry cold snap to her bones, and her spine stiffened, her knuckles turning white against the handle of her suitcase.

The growl of the engine stopped, and the ramp banged against the wooden dock with a loud thud, grating as the waves lifted and lowered the vessel. The man beside her cringed as if the sound had reverberated through his skull. Probably had a bitch of a hangover. Served him right. She tasted bitterness, as cold as the glint in his eyes, but she loaded the kind of smile that left a man weak and wanting for something he could never have. *Ever.*

The light struck Nick's eyes like a laser. Not to mention the wattage of Emily's smile. He lowered his sunglasses and obliterated the power of it, near cloaking the dismal day in darkness. She might have flashed her pearly whites, but he knew animosity when he saw it. The last thing he needed was a confrontation with Charliese's closest friend. The open wound in her chocolate eyes told him loud and clear she believed him responsible for her friend's death.

He *was* responsible. The knowledge crushed his chest and he struggled to draw breath. Loss scraped his already raw nerve endings. The day before had marked the two-year anniversary of Charliese's death. *And* it turned out... *the death of his child.*

He'd put off visiting her gravestone. At first, because he was in hospital recovering from his injuries. Later, because he couldn't face the cold, hard truth of it. Now the words etched into the cold, hard stone were etched into his brain—gouged into the cold, hard flesh of his heart. He'd killed not only his wife, but his child. Why hadn't Charliese told him she was pregnant?

Because she'd planned to divorce him, and the child *wasn't* his? Or because she'd planned to divorce him, and the child *was* his?

He'd never know the truth, but it took his self-loathing and amped it up a thousand-fold. Too much alcohol, the fist fight...nothing relieved the fresh agony of it.

He eyed the woman beside him. Slender, willowy slim and exotic in her designer clothes. Brown doe-like eyes. Pouty, perfect lips and a heart-shaped face that looked both vulnerable and bombshell at the same time. He grappled for the anger that had prompted him to text her. She'd left her family in the lurch while she swanned around the world… and damn it, they needed her. He crushed the thought and took a steadying breath.

"Do you need help with that?" He nodded towards Emily's uber-expensive suitcase. Any man with a pulse would fall over himself to rush to her rescue and give her whatever she asked for *and* feel grateful for the opportunity. *Almost* any man with a pulse.

Blood hammered in his ears and he shifted his gaze. She was a freaking goddess—far from the wild child who used to run around the island in bare feet, in cahoots with her sister. A woman no doubt used to getting what she wanted. She'd bring men to their knees. Weaker men. Men less broken. She was as out of place in this damp, isolated part of the world as a clownfish amongst the local toadies and flathead. He eyed the murky green depths of the water where it slapped against the side of the ferry and forced air into the tightness of his lungs.

"No, thanks. I'm fine." Emily's smile was confident and self-assured, but he could see the damn thing was heavy. Her arms strained to lift it and she plonked it down again while she waited to disembark.

"Here, let me take it." Nick bent forward to pick up her suitcase and near lost his balance when the boat pitched—like the lumpy mattress he'd poured himself into the night before. He tightened his grip on the solid leather handle, but everything else was shifting sand. The ramp dipped up and down and did its best to fling him into the sea. Perhaps a good dousing was what he needed, but the mere thought of the water closing over his head was enough to make his skin prickle in panic. He'd learned to live with it and that was something. He stepped onto the relative stability of the pier and turned back to help her. That smile of hers was lethal and her eyes had the power to turn a man into a pillar of salt or a whimpering slave. She was dynamite, but he wasn't fool enough to care.

She moved past him, and he got a waft of sweet-and-spice. A waft that brought memories, thick and fast. Of beautiful women and a life, long dead.

Emily's suitcase weighed a damn tonne and he couldn't imagine any of it was appropriate for winter on French Island. They walked the length of the pier in silence. He eyed the carpark where his grouchy man-ute—a late-model Toyota Hilux, strong enough and mean enough to face the potholes and corrugations on the local roads—waited in the mud accompanied by a small collection of rusting vehicles. No sign of Beverley's white Suzuki Swift.

"Is your mum coming to pick you up?"

"I thought so, but I don't see her." A gust of wind whipped her hair across her face, but not before he saw the desolation in her eyes.

"Would you like a lift?" Hell, no. What made him go and ask that? The last thing he needed was the scent of a woman lingering on his upholstery. Besides, there was a good chance he was under the influence and the next-to-last thing he needed was another woman's death on his hands. And he saw it in her eyes. That careful assessment. That figuring between the worse of two evils.

"I guess you're headed my way. If it's not too much of an

inconvenience, that would be great. Mum must have gotten side-tracked."

If she was *his* daughter, he'd leave her to walk, too. Superior, haughty and too beautiful for her own good. "Your mum will be relieved to see you."

"She's not well, but I guess you know that. Everyone knows everyone's business here." Her gaze shifted to the mud between the wet wooden boards of the pier and his vehicle. Potholes filled with brown watery muck. Muck that splashed onto a man's vehicle and left it looking like a rally car.

Did she want him to lay down his jacket, so she could walk on that? "I'll pick you up over here if you like."

"Thank you. That's very thoughtful."

"You might want to invest in a pair of gumboots." His tone wasn't friendly, and he didn't give a rat's arse. He lifted her precious suitcase and stormed over to his vehicle, bright blue under the mud, his waterproof hiking boots meeting the muck with a slap. He put her suitcase in the back and made room for her highness in the front passenger seat.

Just being neighbourly, he muttered. Five minutes, tops. He could endure five minutes. Five minutes wasn't long, then he could pull down his blinds and blot out the world.

One minute was too long. From the moment he closed her door and prowled back to sit behind the wheel—his mother had brought him up to be a gentleman and when it came to women, he used his manners—he was excruciatingly aware of her long, slender thighs and the warmth of her beside him. There was that sweet, spicy scent with a hint of salt, like her hair had been infused by the sea. He wanted to hate her. He wanted to be impervious to all that she represented. He wanted to reject her before she could reject him, but there was something about her, something vulnerable, which was ridiculous.

"How do you make a living here, now that you've ditched your acting career?"

"I run the farm."

"Ah." She nodded and looked out the side window.

"What about you? Is the modelling business treating you well?" He navigated a large pothole with only a fraction less than his usual expertise, but the sharp deviation of the vehicle forced her towards him. She reached out to brace herself against the movement. Her left hand—golden, slender and devoid of rings. He didn't care one way or the other. Her fingernails were a soft pink and perfectly polished and hell, look at the road, man. His wheels caught in the soft sand built up at the side of the road and the steering wheel pulled sharply to the left. He reacted a fraction late, but pulled out of the slide, his heart bouncing in his chest, the vehicle slamming into the corrugations. They weren't far from the cross and browning flowers that marked the tree where Chris, a local teen, had sped into a slide and hadn't been able to correct in time. It wasn't like he cared if he ended up wrapped around a tree, but he had a lady in his vehicle.

"Yes, although it takes me away a lot, but I'm here for the foreseeable future."

She said *here* like it was the arse-end of the earth. It shouldn't have come as a surprise. She no doubt liked attention and lots of it. That killer smile was practiced and polished and men the world over probably jerked off to her picture. He doused the bitter thought. Not all beautiful women were like Charliese. "You have bigger and better plans?"

"Don't you?"

She turned her chocolate gaze towards him, and he felt it

like silk against his damaged skin. "No. I couldn't be happier."

"You don't look happy."

"I like my privacy. I like my home. I like my job." He didn't like rescuing precious princesses from the mud or from themselves. He eyed the broken French Island General Store sign that rested on the grass in front of the fibro-cement building. When the hell would Marge and Bob get around to remounting that thing? He made a mental note to put it on his job list and took a deep breath of the fresh air that blew in from the open vent, pungent with the scent of the Cyprus pines, lined up like soldiers, wind-swept and battle-scarred. He fought the nausea and the pounding throb in his head. Three minutes and counting.

"You don't miss LA? The parties. The buzz of the set?"

"No." And he looked after what was his. At least, he did *now*. He'd learned the hard way about what was important, but he'd been there for his mum, which was something. Unlike the woman who sat next to him, who'd left her mother and sister to struggle alone while she lived the good life. High-end clothing. Holier-than-thou attitude.

"You don't feel lonely? It's very isolated here."

Temper twisted through him like the wind howling through the trees. He lowered the window and took a bracing breath of the sharp, cold air, ripe with the scent of cow manure from the open paddocks. "I like my own company. Besides, I keep busy."

"It must be hard to meet women when you live on a near-deserted island."

Her words cut like a blade and his temper stirred like a cantankerous old genie shut in a lamp for a millennium. "If I wanted to date, which I don't, there is this thing called the internet. We do have Wi-Fi out here in the wilderness, even if we don't have mains water."

And if she was fishing to see if he had a new love-interest, she could think again. No woman wanted damaged goods and he couldn't care less. He didn't need a woman; he had a dog, and his dog didn't care what he looked like.

One thousand corrugations and a hundred years later, he pulled up in front of the gate to the While Away B&B and turned to his passenger. "Let me know if you need a lift back to the ferry." Damn, he'd promised Carmen he'd join them for dinner. And meeting Emily again? The timing couldn't have been worse. But she'd probably only while away a weekend before she scurried back to the shine of the big city with its manicures and adoring men. And he didn't care a Black Angus what she thought of him.

She reached for the door handle, before turning her danger-ous gaze back to his. "Thank you for letting me know they needed me. Mum fired Julia without telling me. And I didn't know she was sick."

His muscles contracted. His gut knotted. His skin tightened like a vice. Be anything, but don't be friendly. He didn't deserve it.

"That's okay."

"I miss Charliese. Even now."

Her gaze connected with his, and he felt it like a forcefield or a siren's call. Come close and I'll break you. No thanks, he was broken enough.

"I'm sorry, Emily." He paused, the past wedged between them like cold, hard quartz. "We all make mistakes that we live to regret."

"Not all of us live to regret them." Emily's tone was cold and there was no sign of that high-wattage smile. Now it was gone, he kind of missed it. Despite the glare.

He opened his door and pulled himself free of the bone-chilling blast.

With a cuss at every step, he stomped around to remove Emily's suitcase from the back of the ute. Every footfall sent an answering pang to his temple. He lowered it to the muddy ground and refused to consider her trek from the gate along the crushed-stone driveway. She'd have to carry it—the wheels were as useless here as they'd been on the pier—but that wasn't his problem. *She* wasn't his problem. If she was fool enough to wear that kind of footwear and bring that kind of luggage, then so be it.

"Thanks for the lift." Her tone was velvet-coated steel and she turned away with a snap of her ponytail. Her suitcase wheel got caught in the muck and she used both hands to drag it.

He got the message loud and clear.

She didn't need any man to come to her rescue. Especially not him.

Chapter Two

Emily tiptoed around the puddles and lugged her suitcase towards the distressed wood of the front door. The rustic house was charming. Mud brick with exposed timber beams and local stone. The porch light was on, which was a welcome of sorts. She dropped her suitcase onto the veranda and rubbed her neck. She was used to men rushing to help, not dumping her at a farm gate and leaving her to fend for herself.

She turned to see he was gone. Good. She wasn't sure what she'd find inside. She didn't cope well with vomit. Olfactory memories hit her in waves and her throat contracted. She took deep gulps of air and blew it out slowly, forcing the jittery sensation in her muscles to ease. The door was unlocked, and she pushed through, calling out.

Nothing.

No one.

The smell of fresh apple pie brought a softer surge of memories along with relief. It was a good sign. She left her suitcase in the short hallway and headed into the kitchen, where she found a holy mess. Dirty dishes were stacked in the sink and across the bench. There was flour and debris from the apple pie construction all over the table. Apple peels lay in a stack like browning spaghetti. Clothes were slung over the backs of chairs and there was a teetering stack of unopened mail on the end of the table. The underlying scent in the kitchen came from the over-full bin, a ripe, pungent smell that suggested it hadn't been emptied any time recently. Gone was the scent of turps and oil paint she associated with home. Her mother's paintings—landscapes and seascapes—hung from the mud walls, but they were paintings she recognised. None were new. Even Carmie's paintings, which looked like a kindergartener's rendition of flowers with cheerful splashes of colour, were familiar. She eyed the tracks of dried mud on the wooden boards of the floor and the build-up of dust.

Her gaze shifted to the gaping black grill in the fireplace and the empty wood box, before settling on the incongruent splash of colour—plump pink camellias in a wonky handmade, ceramic vase in the centre of the wooden coffee table. She'd made it in primary school. Camellias were her favourite flowers. Carmie's, too. Along with wild daisies. Emily smiled as she remembered making daisy chains with her older sister. How she'd pushed the head of one flower through the stem of another while Carmie held the growing chain with great care and egged her on. *Another one. Another one.* The kitchen clock ticked with a loud throb in the silence and the space glowed with the orange light of several salt lamps. Several more lacked illumination. No doubt the globes had blown.

Emily heard the joey first. It skittered into the kitchen, all feet and long tail. His hopping movement froze to a frightened ear flicker when he saw her. Behind, with a gleeful laugh, she heard Carmie. The sound brought a smile to her lips, and suffused her body with love and hope. She'd forgotten how much joy her sister exuded. Oh, to have the brain of a seven-year-old and to live in the never-ending magic of childhood.

"E-Em!"

Her sister was heavyset and adoring. She knocked a chair over as she rushed forward and wrapped her arms around Emily in a hug so tight, Emily grunted, the air forced from her lungs. Joey hopped over, his muddy paws and sharp claws snagging on her jeans as he wrapped his arms around her thigh. She couldn't stop the laugh. "Carmie. Joey. I've missed you both." She held her sister close, her nose puckering at the smell of her oily hair, which hadn't been washed in a good while.

"We missed you, too." The s-sounds in her speech were a messy 'th'.

The familiar inflection and booming volume made Emily's heart swell in her chest until the ache was all she could feel. She ruffled Joey's big, furry ears. "Where's Mum?"

"She was tired. She went to bed. We made pie."

"It smells amazing." Emily eyed the timer. Three minutes to go. What if she hadn't arrived? Would it have burned to a crisp while her mother slept? Who was keeping Carmie safe? It was like the planes of time shifted and she slipped back a decade or more. Her old self stepped out of the shadows and her new self was gone. Like shedding one skin and stepping into another. A skin that settled around her like cling wrap, too tight and too restrictive at first, but with Carmie in her arms, the hum of tension eased, and her pulse settled. "You're wet!"

"It was raining before. We played in the puddles."

"Would you like a hot chocolate?" Was there any milk? Emily stepped over to the stainless-steel fridge and checked. Someone had ensured there was food. The basics at least.

"Yes!" Carmie clapped her hands, her face filled with delight.

Emily helped Carmie out of her coat and took a towel from

the hall cupboard. She dried Carmie's hair and then her own. The buzzer throbbed in the kitchen and she grinned. "Shall we have pie?"

"Yes!" Carmie's face lit up, her smile wide.

Emily couldn't help catching it and smiling, too. Joey bounced around the kitchen before disappearing into a fleece-lined bag that hung over the back of a kitchen chair, like a man-made pouch. His head popped up for a short moment before he buried himself in its depths for a nap.

"With ice cream?"

"Yes!"

"We'd better keep quiet or we'll wake Mum."

"She's awake."

Emily turned to see her mother, pale and frail, leaning against the door frame.

"I'm so sorry, darling. I just saw the time. I must have slept through the alarm. It took about a week's worth of energy to make the pie. It knocked me for six."

"Oh, Mum. You look terrible."

"I feel terrible, hon, but it's so good to see you. Welcome home."

"Nick gave me a lift." Emily walked over and gave her mum a hug. She breathed in the familiar scent of her soap—orange and cinnamon—so at least she was clean. But it was the lack of scent that loosened the knot inside of her, a constriction of childhood memories... of coming home from school to a mother who reeked of alcohol. Even so, the woman in her arms was thin, too thin, and her bones protruded through her skin.

"We'd be lost without him. He's helped out more and more since I got sick. Carmie asked him over for dinner. I hope that's okay. I know how you feel about him, but what's done is done. Let's get that pie out of the oven. I want to hear about your travels and I've got about five minutes in me."

Emily's appetite for pie vanished with the sharp contraction in her gut. Wheatley was coming here for dinner? Fabulous. Emily watched her mother stagger to a chair and shock obliterated the rest. She was weak and her balance was off. "I'll get it, Mum. You sit down."

"Thanks, love. I can't stand for long. Even sitting, I get lightheaded."

"How are you functioning? You look like you're in pain. You've lost weight."

"In small bursts. Carmie helps."

"Carmie made the pastry," her sister said with a grin.

"I would have come home sooner if I'd known." Emily reached for the oven mitts. "Why did you fire Julia and why didn't you tell me you were sick?"

"She lorded it over me. I couldn't stand her for another minute, and I didn't want to bother you. I thought we'd get someone else, but I couldn't find anyone, and I couldn't cope on my own, so we stopped taking guests."

"What about the shopping?" Emily pulled the oven door open and waited for the blast of heat to subside. She reached in and took the pie in her mitted hands, then rested it on the hotplates. She slipped the mitts off and closed the oven door, twisting the temperature gauge back to zero.

"Nick's been doing it for us. I give him a list. I'm too dizzy for the barge-ride and the drive to Cranbourne."

"Nick gave us flowers." Carmie pointed to the centre of the small coffee table. "He said camellias remind him of Carmie."

"And he's dropped a meal in every day since he found out

28

Julia was gone and saw how sick I was," her mum added. "He headed over to the mainland yesterday, but he left lamb cutlets and vegies for last night, and lasagne and salad for tonight. It's in the fridge."

"He didn't look too good this morning." That was an understatement and she struggled to equate the man they described with the man who had killed her best friend. "You make him sound like a saint."

Carmie nodded, a dreamy smile on her face. Carmie had a crush on him? Of course, she did. He'd brought her flowers. Did he even know what he'd done? Emily's fury ignited and caught flame. How dare he. How dare he create hopes and wishes and fantasies in her sister's heart. Foolish man. Stupid, thoughtless, inconsiderate cretin. Carmie would be hurt when he did what all men did. Leave, without a care or a look back over his shoulder.

"Well, I'm here now. Would you like tea with your pie?" She took the electric kettle and filled it with water.

"Yes, love. Thanks."

"And ice cream." Carmie's eyes shone.

"Sounds good to me. It's never too early for ice cream." Emily's smile belied the bitterness that coiled inside her like a snake. She found bowls in the cupboard beneath the granite bench and pulled them out. She walked the short distance to the freezer, where she found a tub of vanilla ice cream.

The pie was golden with caramelised sugar and the knife crunched through the crispy pastry into plump steaming apple, the scent of cinnamon, pungent and delicious. Emily cut huge servings with two scoops of ice-cream and tried not to think of how far she'd need to run to get rid of the calories. She was home and right now she wished she'd never left, but it was her work that paid the mortgage. It was her work that injected oxygen into her veins and breathed life into her soul.

Carmie devoured the pie like she hadn't eaten for six weeks. Emily couldn't hide the grin. She sometimes envied her sister. She took a huge mouthful and savoured the familiar flavours, the simple pleasure of apple pie and ice cream.

Her mother struggled to eat and consumed less than a blowfly, of which there were many, buzzing at the windows, desperate to get out. Emily watched her mother with growing concern. She was wasting away, and her skin had a grey tinge to it.

"When did you see the doctor last?"

"I was too sick to go over on the barge, but he visits here once a month. I'll see him next week."

"How much weight have you lost?"

"A few kilograms."

More like ten. Worry wormed its way into her heart. "You're skin and bone."

"Eating exhausts me. Breathing exhausts me. Sleeping exhausts me."

"I wish I'd known. I would have come home sooner."

"I know, honey, but I didn't want to worry you and I thought it would pass. I thought I'd overdone it and needed to rest, but no amount of rest is enough."

"What did the doctor say?"

"To manage the symptoms. Gentle exercise. Counselling. I just have to ride it out."

"What about alternative medicine? Acupuncture? Diet?"

"I don't have the energy to read up about it. I fought it for the first month, but now, I just try to get through each day." She sagged against the chair, deflating like a sail turned into the wind. Emily watched in horror. She looked like an old woman, sucked dry by life. Thin, faded, and dull.

"Sleeping during the day must mess with your sleep at night. You look tired, Mum. Exhausted." Emily's heart thundered in her ears and her pulse ebbed and flowed. Her mum was sick, really sick, and Nick had been right to demand she come home.

"I wake up in the night, then can't get back to sleep."

"What about your painting?"

"I haven't done any."

"The vegie garden?"

"Gone to seed, but the pumpkins self-sowed so we have those." Her mother's voice trailed off. "I need to get back to bed."

"Here, I'll help you." Emily took her mum's arm and half-carried her back to the darkened bedroom.

"I had to put the guests off, love. I wasn't up for it."

"I understand." Emily pulled up the covers and tucked her mother in. Her eyes were already closed, her forehead scrunched like her head throbbed. Emily lowered her hand to her mother's brow. Her skin felt cold and clammy. Emily pressed the bedclothes closer around her. Already her breathing was soft and regular, like she'd fallen asleep the moment her head touched the pillow.

Emily tiptoed from the room. She'd known from a young age that Carmie was *her* responsibility. Her mother wasn't the kind of woman who managed life. Life managed her. When their father left, Emily grew up. She cooked dinner. She washed the dishes afterwards. She forced her mother to eat when her own food stuck in her throat. She salvaged what she could from her mother's meagre welfare cheque. She walked Carmie to school. She helped Carmie with her homework and she never, never forgot. Never would a man do to her what her father had done to her mother. Never would she seek solace in a bottle and leave her children to fend for themselves. Never would she forget the smell of alcohol and vomit.

Bitterness rose and fell, and Emily pulled the door shut.

Nick cut the engine and sat for a long moment, wondering how he'd let Carmie cajole him into joining them for dinner. Carmie spoke of her younger sister like she was an angel with big, shiny wings and a halo to match. More like a precious princess with a thorny crown. Still, company was better than silence, and the silence in his own home rang loud in his ears. It tolled like a bell. It suffocated and crushed.

He reached for the bottle of wine, and the bag of carrots, cauliflower, and spinach from the garden. The wind caught his door and it slammed shut, lethal like the chop of an axe, but there was no going back. He lifted the latch and pushed through the gate. Where usually his feet were light and brisk across the crushed-stone driveway, today they dragged. Where usually his heart was open and filled with the simple pleasure of connecting with his neighbours, today he lumbered across the short distance like a hulking bear. Where usually he longed for the warmth and laughter that blossomed inside his neighbour's house like roses in the sunshine, today the mud walls seemed to shun him.

He couldn't disappoint Carmie. A promise was a promise, but the promise didn't sit well on his shoulders. It sat heavy and awkward and cumbersome. Emily *Stone*. Her name brought boulders to mind and the crushing weight of water over his head. Funny how Carmie's name turned his mind to shiny pebbles and childhood treasures. He shifted the weight of the bag in his arms and his grip tightened on the bottle of wine.

The cottage loomed out of the dank grey of the late afternoon, the veranda light glowing like a beacon. The grass was overgrown and lush—rich green and vibrant. The wind pulled and buffeted. The open sea was down there, beyond the manna and swamp gums, the salty scent a constant, along with the rhythmic surge and suck of the waves. A gull shrieked and wheeled overhead, making his heart leap and bang in his chest. He took a deep breath of the damp, earthy air and with it came the rich scent of garlic and hearty cooking. It wrapped around him like a soft, soft throw and his heart swelled. Memories. Memories of his mother's cooking. Coming in from the farm with his dad, his muscles burning, his heart full. Now, when he came in from the paddocks—alone—the house was dark and empty. The thought was like salt to an open wound. He lifted his knuckles to knock on the door, but it peeled back, and a human cannonball leapt into his already full arms.

"Nick! You're here. What took you so long?"

"Hey, sweet cheeks. Help me out here."

Carmie peeked into the bag. "Vegies!"

"Yep. From the garden."

"Come on. We kept you some apple pie." She dragged him into the warmth and slammed the door behind him.

"My favourite."

The scent of lasagne was stronger now and the home-and-hearth goodness tugged at his heart. Salt lamps glowed like precious gems.

"Emily! Nick's here."

Her speech was a jumble of words, the "s's" more of a "th," but Nick had gotten good at deciphering it. He could hear the crackle and hiss of an open fire as a log shifted and collapsed, and the warm glow of the kitchen drew him onwards, down the short hallway lined with photographs and pictures of a young Carmie and Emily, sometimes together, their arms wrapped around each other, sometimes alone. Carmie's face was an open delight, Emily's smile more guarded. What was it like for her, growing up with an older sister who had Down syndrome? She'd clearly left at the first opportunity, too busy with her own glamorous, model existence to care about the family she'd left behind.

She was here now.

Too little, too late. Poor Bev had struggled for weeks. How would Carmie have coped if he hadn't discovered their plight by chance? She wasn't capable of caring for her mother, and Bev was past caring for anyone.

Carmie's grip was strong and oblivious to his heel-digging resistance. He plastered a smile on his freshly shaved face for Carmie's sake, but it was rickety and of poor workmanship and the moment he laid eyes on Emily, it slipped to the floor and shattered. She was at the sink washing dishes in a pair of low crotch track pants and a soft cashmere top, the sleeves pulled up, her hands lost in pink rubber gloves. Her blonde hair was pulled back into a high ponytail and she looked like a freaking angel.

"Hi again." She half-turned to welcome him and he grappled for the smile.

"Thanks for having me over." His gut twisted as he lowered the vegies and wine onto the table. "From the garden and the local vineyard." He eyed the camellias in their wonky vase and his heart turned in his chest, the weight of it aching. They were his mother's favourite and they'd bloomed big and beautiful this year as if she'd tended them from afar.

He shifted his attention to Carmen, and the game of snakes and ladders she'd set up on the coffee table by the fire. The wood box held a small pile of wood, neatly stacked. The fire breathed warmth and light into the tidy space. It was like someone had waved a magic wand and created a home. Gone was the mess of yesterday and the smell of decay.

"Come on. I'm green. You're red." Carmie threw the die. Her short hair shone, and her smile was radiant. She wore black pants and a sparkly silver cardigan over a white shirt embossed with tiny flowers. Her lips shone with a soft pink gloss, like magic had transformed her.

"Red's faster. Everyone knows that." Nick shucked out of his coat and wrapped it around one of the kitchen chairs. "You look very pretty."

"That's what Em said." Carmie flashed him a happy smile, which faltered when she saw his eye. "What happened to your eye?" She studied him, oblivious to the fact she was staring.

"It copped a bruising."

"Does it hurt?"

He wanted to say, like a bitch, but he was in company. "It sure does." Thank God the throb in his head had eased. "Let's get on with the game. Unless you're scared I'm going to beat you."

"Nope," Carmie said with a laugh. "I'm going to beat you." She picked up the die and gave it a toss. "Yes," she yelled with delight. "Five." She moved her piece forward five places and shot up a ladder. "Your turn."

Nick settled into the leather chair opposite her. The warmth of the fire soothed and calmed and coaxed the knots from his muscles. "Okay. Get ready to be impressed." He shook the die with dramatic fanfare, and it landed on one.

"One?" Carmie's tone took his bravado and stomped on it.

"Every move counts." He handed the die over with a grin. He became aware of the soft sound of Mozart behind the clink of the dishes as Emily worked in the kitchen. "Where's Joey?"

"He's sleeping. So is Mum."

Nick tried to keep his focus on the game and ignore the way his body tuned in to Emily's every move. When she approached with a glass of wine, it was like a sensor went off and every part of him flashed an alert. Danger. Hazard. Bunker down. The knots were back, fiercely clenched.

"Thank you." His gaze shifted from the action on the board to the woman whose scent reminded him of the wildflowers that thrived on the island in spring. Her eyes shone with something he couldn't fathom. Sadness? Joy? Love? Hate? All of the above? He took the glass, his hand trembling. He'd slept the day away and stood under the shower for half an hour, the hot water drumming life into his limbs. He'd scrubbed up okay, considering he felt like death at the edges.

"Dinner smells amazing."

"Thank you, for making it. Thank you, for taking care..." Her words cut off as if they'd snagged in her throat or the need to say thanks had caused her to gag.

"They needed help." He couldn't keep the accusatory note from his tone or the hard knot from balling in his stomach.

"They did." She turned away.

He'd expected a barrage of excuses, empty and excessive. What he got was an honest answer and an eyeful of glorious woman. His gaze followed the sway of her hips, her slender waist. Her ponytail shone like spun silk and his fingers prickled with the desire to touch it. When was the last time he'd seen such an attractive woman? So long his body seemed to react of its own accord. This was Emily. Charliese's best friend. Carmie's younger sister. Not a woman he wanted to find attractive. He rubbed his hands on his thighs as if the unwanted sensation could be wiped away. A sheen of sweat broke out on his brow and he shuffled back in his seat to invite distance from the warmth of the flames.

"Six!" The word was a tricky one for her to pronounce, but Carmie's tone was triumphant. She slipped her token up the ladder to the top row.

Nick was getting beaten and he couldn't have been happier about it. He sipped his wine and pondered the board. He needed a four. He threw the die and landed a three.

Some days things didn't go the way you wanted them to. He slid his token down the snake's slippery skin and found himself back on the second row.

Some days didn't go the way you expected them to. He'd expected to dislike the woman who'd neglected her family while she swanned around the world, adored and spoiled.

And some days didn't go the way you planned. He'd planned to give her a piece of his mind, but his thoughts, his feelings, his temper were knotted and gnarled. It made no sense. His mind couldn't get a grip. His thoughts careened and clashed.

This woman was light and warmth and comfort.

This woman might look like a princess, dress like a princess, act like a princess, but she was up to her elbows in suds washing up more than a day's worth of dishes. The house was tidy and sparkly, and it smelled good, like she'd opened the windows and chased away the stale. Carmie looked good, too. Dressed up and far from the dirty urchin he'd come across a few weeks ago.

This woman called to him in a myriad of ways… ways he fully planned to ignore.

"Dinner's ready when you are. Finish him off, Carmie."

Carmie took the die and threw it halfway across the room in her excitement. She raced after it. "Yay! A two. I win!" She danced a jig and raced over to hug Emily, who hugged her close.

"Great job. Now, let's eat. I've worked up an appetite. You and Nick pack up, while I go and wake Mum."

Carmen raced over to move her piece and squealed with excitement. "I won. I won."

Nick held out his hand for a high five. "Well done. I couldn't beat you, not even with the colour advantage."

"Nope." Her brown eyes lit with pure joy.

"Who taught you to play so well?"

"Em."

"Ah." Curiouser and curiouser. He helped Carmie pack up the board and sat back to study the flames. The wine loosened the barbs from his thoughts, enough for him to question his judgement. Emily, it seemed, was more than he'd assumed.

"Em made garlic bread. I like garlic bread."

"Me, too." Em wasn't an angel. She was a magician. She'd created a home. A warm, inviting, comfortable home. Every breath inflated his lungs with more than oxygen, with something more vital. Emily's love for her sister was tangible in every word, every smile, every action. And that was what appealed the most. He thought of the dark emptiness in his own house. He worked in the paddocks from dawn until late just to avoid being there. Loneliness crouched in the corners. Despair in the cobwebs. Neglect in the dust. He'd spend tomorrow cleaning.

You want to invite her over.

No. No, that wasn't it. That definitely wasn't it.

Then what was it?

This was a home. This was family. This was something special. And he hadn't realised how much he longed for it.

"Come on, Nick. Let's sit at the table. Em put my flowers in the middle."

Nick rose with his glass of wine and reached out his free hand to capture Carmie's. He laughed when she near dragged him across the room. Emily returned at that moment and stilled; her gaze as barbed as a fishhook. What? What had he done? "Where would you like us to sit?"

"Anywhere."

"Okay." Nick lowered his glass to the table. "How's your mum?"

"Not up for dinner." Worry left a tract across her forehead. "She's lost a lot of weight. I'll try her again later."

Emily lowered a plate of steaming lasagne in front of him and a bowl of green salad into the middle of the table. She probably lived on the stuff. There wasn't much of her. Charliese would have complained that pasta was too starchy. A lettuce leaf would have been her entire meal.

Nope. Three plates of lasagne. One for each of them. *And* garlic bread. The smell of garlicky butter made him salivate. He reached for a piece of the crunchy bread, steaming hot from the oven. "Thanks, I love garlic bread."

"It's Carmie's favourite, too."

Emily's tone was gravelly, and it got under his skin, lifting the follicles like an electric charge. He focused on Carmie who chatted and laughed and reacted to his jokes while Emily ate real food like a real person and shared some wine, albeit less than half a glass. He wasn't up for much himself and drank a sip for politeness. The evening filled him with something vital. Something that had been missing. Something he craved.

Emily tucked Carmie into bed and kissed her on the forehead. "I love you, Carmie. Sleep tight, beautiful girl."

"I love you, too, Em." Carmie's voice tapered off as sleep pulled her into its warm, snuggly depths.

Emily smiled as she retreated. What she wanted was a clean kitchen and her own warm bed. What she had was an unwanted guest to deal with. Her muscles ached, sodden and heavy with fatigue, and something sharp throbbed in her left shoulder blade.

What she had, it turned out, was a man up to his elbows in suds and a clean kitchen. Emily stood in the doorway, her mind reeling. "How did you manage that, Wheatley? I wasn't gone for more than ten minutes."

He turned, his body twisting, his hands still in the water. "I know my way around a kitchen, Stone."

His gaze was blue and steady. There was the shiny bruise around his eye. The angry red slash of the scar across his cheek. And that crazy teenage infatuation rose from the ashes and sent a wave of heat to her cheeks. Gone was the cold judgement she'd sensed earlier, but if he thought he could inveigle his way into her good books by being nice to Carmie and helping her out in the kitchen, he was… on the right track. "Would you like a tea? A hot chocolate?"

"Sure. I boiled the kettle. A black tea would be great. Then I need to go. I have an early start tomorrow and you look done in. You must want to get to bed."

She was surprised he'd noticed. Even more surprised he had

an early start. The man Charliese had described didn't rise before noon, hungover and grumpy. "I saw your cattle on the way past this morning. Black Angus? You have a lot."

"Yes. A few hundred. They keep me busy. A tree went down over one of the fences while I was away so tomorrow will see me chain-sawing. Would you like some wood for the fire?" He nodded towards the near-empty wood box.

"Yes, please."

Emily pondered the guy who stood at her sink, all brawn and muscle, his butt kind of tasty in his denim jeans, his big hands tending her dishes. There was something about the wide sweep of his shoulders, the hand-knitted woollen sweater, the way his damp hair curled at his nape. Was it possible for a person to change? This man had killed her best friend—long before her actual death—and she should hate him. She did hate him. Her stomach tightened and her body heated, but not with a searing flash of anger. She reached into the cupboard and found a couple of porcelain mugs, fine enough for tea, but big enough for more than a mouthful. She flicked the switch on the kettle, and it sprang into life.

"Sugar?"

"Nope. I'm sweet enough."

She smirked. "Since when?" He couldn't have appeared more different from the aggrieved scrap of human debris she'd met that morning or the selfish narcissist her friend had planned to divorce. Maybe the accident had knocked some sense into him or some ego out of him.

"You're not the woman I thought you were."

And you're not the man I thought you were. She kept that thought to herself, her brow puckering. "Who did you think I was?"

"The selfish princess-type who was too busy with her own life to care for her family."

That was rich coming from him. The kettle screamed as the water bubbled and banged against its metal sides. Emily dropped teabags into the cups and poured boiling water over them. "What makes you think I'm not?"

"Carmie." He lifted the ceramic lasagne dish out of the water and rinsed it off.

"When it comes to her, I'm more of a mama-bear."

"I get that. If looks could eviscerate, I'd have lost some vital organs." He let the plug out and the water drained away with a loud sucking sound, leaving the sink skirted with suds.

"I think she has a crush on you. You gave her flowers. You called her pretty. I don't want her to get hurt." Emily's muscles clenched and her skin tightened. What rose in her throat had more than claws. It had jagged teeth and a mean attitude.

"Just being a good neighbour." He swept the cloth over the bench, his body big and heated and close.

"Yeah, well that's not how Carmie sees it." She couldn't keep the growl from her tone, and she didn't try. She was pissy and tired, and she had Nick Wheatley in her kitchen. Without conscious thought, she turned the talisman on her right ring finger and took a deep breath. He'd looked after her family. Cooked food for them. Done the shopping. He deserved her civility.

"Perhaps you can't handle sharing the limelight with your sister. I'm sure you're used to getting the lion's share." His tone was jocular, but there was accusation beneath the friendly.

"Perhaps *you* should stop making assumptions. You don't know me at all, which you might have if you'd made any effort to fit into Charliese's life. You were too full of your own ego."

Her pulse pounded in her ears and her breath came short and jagged.

"Perhaps you're right." His movement stilled, and his blue gaze captured hers, turning sapphire.

There was maybe-I'd-like-to-get-to-know-you in the pristine depths and another wave of unwanted warmth washed over her. Her gaze veered to the right side of his face, to the scar that gouged his tanned cheek and pulled the skin there tight, distorting the symmetry of his face. It served him right, but his face was ruined and the hard edges inside of her softened—a smidge. Or maybe it was the raw honesty she'd seen in the depths of his eyes, but when her gaze flicked back to his, the sapphire warmth was gone, and the blue had turned frosty and inhospitable. She stifled the urge to ask about the accident. About the months that followed and his decision to come back to the island. It was a long way from LA and the life he'd lived. Instead, she stayed silent. Any interest in Nick was a betrayal to Charliese and a betrayal to Carmie. She didn't want to mislead him. She wasn't interested in a connection of any kind. "Anyway, I appreciate everything you've done to help out. I owe you big time."

"You don't owe me anything." His tone was dead flat and icy, like it had gotten too close to those glacier eyes and frozen solid.

And then she realised. Did he think she'd judged his face and found it lacking?

She'd hurt him. It was an awful realisation and before she had time to think, she reached out to console him, to reassure him, to fix it. But the thick, hard muscle beneath her touch threw her off-centre. "That's how the world works." Her cynicism was there, unadorned. It was only fair he knew the lay of the land.

"That's not the way *I* work."

"Touché." She opened a cupboard door and dropped the used teabags into the bin there. "Shall we sit by the fire? Have some chocolate?" He'd been kind to her family, and she found herself torn. Torn between loyalty to Charliese and gratitude. Torn between the desire to crush him and sympathy. Torn between judgement and pity.

"Sure."

The stiffness in his body radiated *no* and the air between them that had been near companionable, became as taut and stretched as the skin on his face. She reached for the dried orange slices she'd brought from the mainland, half-coated in dark chocolate. Tension was like acid in her bones and she fought the bite of it. They needed to get along and she needed him to see the dangers of being overly friendly with Carmie. She didn't want her sister's heart broken, but if Nick disappeared because of something she said, then it would be her fault as much as his. "We need to get along, for Carmie's sake."

He settled a dry tea towel over the dishes in the drainer. "Fine. No problem." He headed to the fireplace and stabbed at the glowing embers until the log fell apart, sending a spray of sparks into the chimney. Flames flared greedily and devoured the fresh wood. The scarred side of his face appeared grotesque with angry shadows.

Emily lowered their tea onto the small table and went back for the chocolate. Picking up her cup, she settled into one of the vintage leather chairs and curled her legs beneath her. She forced herself to relax or to at least appear relaxed, for in truth, her muscles and joints and bones were in gridlock.

"You've had a busy day. I barely recognise the place." His voice was carefully controlled, and he gulped his tea like he wanted this little soirée done and dusted.

"Mum wasn't well enough to stay on top of it." She eyed him over the rim of her cup. "I'm glad I'm back." And she was. Like stepping into an old pair of slippers or comfy track pants. Like letting go of that part of her that played at being glamorous, like a kid tottering around in high heels.

"You were gone a long time."

She got the thrust in his undertone. "Two months, but you're right. I've been booked solid, which is good, because the B&B hasn't been. But I need to get back more often."

"I read chronic fatigue can take a long time to recover from."

How will they manage when you pack up and leave? Again.

Emily got the question loud and clear and resented it. "Yes. I read that, too." She bit her lower lip. There was a limit to how long she could drop her life without losing it altogether. She'd put money aside, but the B&B barely kept them afloat and she had to make hay while the sun shone… perhaps that was an analogy he could understand. Modelling was a time-limited career. She didn't have the luxury of saying no, thanks.

"How will they manage?"

"I'll organise a new manager for the B&B. Someone who can look after Carmie and Mum." There was desolation in her tone and a crushing vice around her chest. She rushed to disguise it with a sip of her tea. She'd prefer to be here herself, but it wasn't possible.

Nick lowered his cup and stared at the flames.

The bad side of his face was towards her and Emily's thoughts returned to the accident. He'd lost more than his wife. He'd lost his life or the life he'd known. The man he'd been. *Don't feel sorry for him. He doesn't deserve it. Charliese lost her life. The life of her child.* But he'd been there for Emily's family when she hadn't. "Life can throw some curve balls, can't it?"

"It sure can."

His gaze shifted to hers then dropped to her hands, where they wrapped around her cup. His body stiffened and his brow creased. Charliese's ring. Emily stuffed her right hand into her pocket. Hell, she'd forgotten about that. He must have recognised it. She should have taken it off, but she'd promised Charliese she would wear it and her promise to her friend was more important than Nick's ego. Or at least it had been.

"I'd better go. I've got an early start." There was awkwardness in his movement, like his joints had fused. He rubbed his palms on the front of his jeans before settling his hands into his pockets. "Thank you for the lovely dinner."

"Thank *you* for the lovely dinner. Do you need some help with the tree tomorrow? I'm sure I could do something."

"That's a kind offer. I'll let you know." His tone told her she wouldn't be hearing from him any time soon. The volume of his voice lowered to a soft murmur as they moved into the hallway. "I'll drop the wood over when I'm done."

An image of him flashed into her mind—his axe held high, his muscles ripped, the sun shining on his tanned back—and it near took her breath away. "That would be great. Thanks." He pushed through the doorway and out into the night.

Emily stood on the veranda, the rush of cold air like a slap to her cheeks. A myriad of scents told her she was home. The eucalyptus, the salt, the earthy scent of the ground. The sky was filled with a trillion stars—so many more visible here than in the city—and the moon was full and bright. It was quiet and hushed, and the silence stretched awkwardly between them.

The damage to Nick's face was vivid. The cruel gash. The shiny bruise around his eye. He stood motionless, his hands in his pockets, his shoulders ruched up like the muscles in his neck were pulled tight. A possum squealed and Emily shivered, wrapping her arms around her body.

"Right. I'd better be off." His eyes glinted in the moonlight and his chest lifted like he had something to say, but then he shook his head and turned towards the gate.

"Goodnight," Emily called, her hand on the door.

"I'll be in touch to see how your mum's faring."

Emily watched as he trudged towards the gate, his back curved against the cold. The thought of him alone, entirely alone, wasn't as appealing as it should have been.

Chapter Three

"Ah, excuse me, mate. Could you point me in the direction of Mosquito Creek Road?"

Nick eyed the expensive suit, the tanned face, the white-toothed smile. So, this was the pilot of the helicopter he'd spied in Bob's paddock beside the general store. There weren't too many folks who didn't take the ferry or the barge. The guy had a folded-up map of the island in one hand and the other was lifted to shade his eyes from the winter sun. There was a chill in the air and every breath left a cloud of fog between them.

"Where are you headed?" Nick's tone was casual, but there was nothing casual about the way his muscles contracted and ticked. Besides, he already knew the answer. There was only one person this kind of man could be here to visit. There wasn't much on Mosquito Creek Road besides the odd farm and the While Away B&B.

"I'm here to see a friend, Emily Stone. Well, she's more of a girlfriend—ex-girlfriend—I guess."

Ex-girlfriend? The guy was old enough to be her father, which was rich coming from him. He was seven years older than Emily and it hadn't stopped him from feeling something… attraction. What man wouldn't be attracted to her? She was dynamite, but he wasn't interested.

He didn't have to be interested to want to protect her. And if this fellow was her ex, then what the hell was he doing here?

A week had passed since Nick made his awkward farewell. The ring he'd seen on her right hand perplexed him still. It couldn't be a coincidence. It had to be the one he'd given Charliese for their engagement. He'd found Charliese's wedding band in the top drawer of their bathroom cabinet, discarded amongst their toothbrushes and toothpaste, but he hadn't found her diamond ring. Why had she given it to Emily? The question had haunted him for a week. He'd found himself passing their driveway for fictitious reasons, but today he'd finally loaded the back of his ute with firewood and had a legitimate reason to drop in on his neighbours. He'd taken a detour to pick up some takeaway coffees. "I was about to head there myself. Would you like a lift?"

"Sure. That'd be great."

"Are you planning to stay?"

"I booked into the B&B. Thought I'd check it out and follow up some loose ends at the same time."

"Is Emily expecting you?"

"She's expecting a guest."

"Ah." The dangers of three women running a B&B in the middle of nowhere hadn't crossed Nick's mind until that moment. He'd have to find a damn good reason to stay close over the next couple of days, whether Emily liked it or not. Whether *he* liked it or not. His skin crawled with misgivings as he led the way to his ute. "How bad of a break-up was it?"

"It was kind of one-sided, to be honest." The fellow pulled the passenger door open and hoisted his bag onto the floor between his feet.

So, Emily had done the calling off, which morphed Nick's misgivings into concern and his concern into worry. He settled the coffees onto the console and pulled his own door shut behind him.

"There's a lot of wildlife hereabouts. Especially koalas. If you look up in the trees as we pass, you should see one."

"Great."

"What's your name?"

"Phillip. Phillip Campbell."

"I'm Nick Wheatley. I own the farm next door to the B&B on Mosquito Creek Road." He held out his hand and Phillip gave it an insipid shake. His hands were soft, like he used hand creams or something.

"*The* Nick Wheatley? I read about your accident a while back, and your injuries. I used to work with Charliese in the old days. Not so much after the wedding. I was sorry to hear about your loss."

"Yeah, well. That's in the past now." Nick wasn't one for conversation and he saw no point in blabbering, so the trip was a quiet one despite the questions that burned on his tongue. He was glad when he pulled up at the gate to the While Away B&B and could escape the razor-sharp air in the cab of his vehicle. He yanked the gate open and rested it on the chock in the overlong grass, which at ten in the morning, was still iced with frost. Spider webs sparkled in the sun like strands of jewels.

"Nick!" Carmie raced along the driveway with Joey at her heels and threw herself into his arms.

"Your hugs are the best in the world," he said with a grin. Then Emily's words echoed in his head and he rushed to add. "...you're the best friend a man could have. Where's Emily?"

"Inside. She baked scones. With jam and cream. You're just in time."

"I brought coffees. And firewood. And a visitor."

"Who is it?"

Nick turned to see Phillip behind him, his bag in his hand, his face pale and drawn, judgement rippling off him in waves. Had he never seen a person with Down syndrome before? Nick's fists clenched and every muscle knotted in protest. He wanted to pull Carmie behind him and bare his teeth at the threat. No wonder Emily was prickly and defensive. She'd lived with this for years. Instead, he smoothed the sharpness from his tone. "Phillip, this is Carmen, better known as Carmie. Emily's older sister. And Carmie, this is Phillip, a friend of Emily's."

"Hi." Carmie studied Phillip for a long moment and her expression suggested she wasn't impressed. Nick couldn't say he didn't like it.

"Hi… you're Emily's sister?"

The tension in Nick's muscles eased. If Phillip didn't know about Carmie's condition, then he and Emily weren't close. She didn't trust him. Nor did he know her. Not the woman Nick had glimpsed. Not the woman whose love for her sister had left him spinning like a dust mote in a ray of sunshine. Nick was relieved and he didn't take the time to study that too closely.

Emily had surprised him, and he wasn't easily surprised. Not anymore. He realised he'd done the very thing he feared others would do to him. He'd judged her by her appearance. Perhaps that was why he'd stayed away. Or perhaps it was because she was a living, breathing reminder of what he'd done. He'd failed to keep his wife safe. He'd failed to love her enough. If that was Charliese's ring—and he knew it was—it had to be—then

Charliese would have told her the truth. And if Emily knew the truth, she'd know he was even uglier on the inside than he was on the outside and that was something that was hard to face. If it wasn't for Carmie, he wouldn't be here.

"Yes, I'm Emily's sister. Who are you?" Carmie's lisp was worse when she was wound up. She stood with her feet wide, her hands on her hips, and her eyes narrowed.

"Phillip Campbell." He put his hand out to shake hers, but Carmie twisted away and was gone, stumbling back towards the house where Emily stood on the veranda, drying her hands on a towel.

"I'll bring the ute through," Nick said and settled into the cab alone. He watched Phillip stride along the stone driveway, his back straight, his gaze on Emily. Nick's own gaze shifted to where Emily stood with her arm around Carmie, her body rigid. So, she wasn't pleased to see Phillip. Something bloomed in his chest as velvety soft and bountiful as the camellia flowers that lay in the back for Carmie. Not relief. Not desire. Not when that part of his body had died in the accident along with his wife. But attraction. Like a ray of light through storm clouds. She was damn gorgeous, but it was more than that. Charliese had been gorgeous and gorgeous he could live without. What drew him to Emily was the glow of her love for her family. She wore a pale pink apron over a pair of black leather pants and a soft grey top. With her hair pulled back into a ponytail, she looked young and vulnerable. Sophisticated and vulnerable. Gorgeous and vulnerable. Perhaps it was her vulnerability that made his muscles clench, his blood race, his senses become hyperalert. The smell of baking grabbed him the moment he stepped out of the cab.

Emily stood on the porch with her chin lifted like a gladiator princess about to face an opponent. Her gaze was fixed on the man before her. "Phillip. What are you doing here?"

"I needed to speak with you. In person. Not over the phone. I'm sorry about using an assumed name on the booking, but I wasn't sure you'd want to see me."

She pulled Carmie closer. "Did you meet my sister, Carmie?"

"Yes."

"I made some scones. We were expecting you... or Mr. Anderson at least. Come on in."

Nick stepped up beside Phillip. "I found him out by the general store and since I was on my way here..." He faltered, like a cat who'd arrived with a dead mouse in its mouth, only to be greeted with displeasure. "I have that load of firewood in the back. I brought you coffee. Here." This wasn't going well. He handed a takeaway cup over to Emily. "And Miss Carmie, some flowers for you." He passed the flowers over to Carmie, who shrieked with delight.

"I love camellias. My special flower. Thank you, Nick."

"Come on in and have a scone," Emily said, her brow creasing. She didn't like him giving Carmie flowers. He hadn't forgotten, but Carmie's joy was addictive and he'd been hard pressed not to bring them. Not when his garden was full of them and his plants were loaded to the ground.

Phillip turned to him, a steely glint in the grey of his eyes. A muscle ticked in his jaw. Battle lines had been drawn, but he had the picture all wrong.

"Sounds and smells delicious. I'll unload the wood afterwards." Nick pulled his jacket closer around him. "How's your mum?"

"No change. Thanks for the coffee. That was thoughtful."

No thanks for the flowers. She didn't trust him, and the

53

thought cut deeply. He dug his hands deep into his pockets. What girl didn't like to get flowers and why should Carmie miss out? He had no doubt Emily had received her fair share over the years.

"Your mum's not well?" Phillip's expression was dark and confused. "You didn't tell me any of this. I thought we were… close."

This clearly related to Carmie.

"That's why I rushed home. Mum has been diagnosed with chronic fatigue syndrome and the woman I hired to help didn't work out."

"You thought I couldn't handle it?"

Emily's expression suggested exactly that. "You wanted the fairy tale. The fantasy. We're from different worlds."

"You didn't give me a chance."

"I don't like to be disappointed." Her smooth brow creased for a brief moment and Nick saw the flash of pain before she turned towards the door.

Interesting. He followed Phillip into the warmth of the kitchen and breathed the scent of hot scones, freshly removed from the oven. Mozart played in the background and a fire crackled in the grate. Phillip lowered his bag to the floor and his gaze circled the small but comfortable space.

Nick settled himself beside Carmie at the table and took a sip of his coffee. No one made a brew like Marge from the general store. He reached for a scone and spread some jam and whipped cream on it. Golden brown. Fresh from the oven. Heaven to a lonely bachelor.

Emily hadn't shared much of herself with Phillip at all. She hadn't trusted him. The thought was better than the jam and cream. He shifted his neck from side to side and loosened the muscles that had bunched up across his shoulders since he'd come across the fellow.

Carmie tucked into her scones with messy enthusiasm. Phillip's over-white smile was less certain now and his tanned face had lost much of its warmth. He looked out of place in his expensive suit. As out of place as Nick had expected Emily to look. Except Emily didn't look out of place. She sat at the table across from him, her scent sweet, her top soft and snug. He may not be worthy of her, but he was far worthier than this shark, who seemed to have landed from the depths of the sea rather than the open air.

"Help yourself to tea. The pot's hot," Emily said to Phillip.

"Thanks, my dear."

My dear? The two words grated across his skin like metal filings. Phillip was older than Emily and Nick took objection to the way he spoke down to her, like she was a child or stupid. Nick eyed the expensive watch on Phillip's wrist. He was clearly used to getting what he wanted, but right now, what he wanted wasn't too happy to see him. Emily wore a dark scowl on her beautiful face and Nick shouldn't have been enjoying this quite as much as he was.

"I don't think the island will keep you entertained for long, although it's beautiful in its own way," Emily said. "But it doesn't compare to Hamilton or Qualia."

"I'm not here to see the island." There was seduction in his tone, but Emily appeared oblivious.

"There are good photo opportunities though." She shifted her attention to Nick. "Phillip is a photographer. We often work together on fashion shoots."

"French Island is a long way from Milan," Nick said, and made no effort to hide his animosity. He sank his teeth into another scone and sat back to enjoy it.

"That it is, but she's worth it."

"She makes a mean scone, that's for sure." Nick gazed across at Emily. The corner of her mouth tweaked like a smile threatened, but there was brevity in her eyes.

"Who wants to play snakes and ladders?" Carmie's eyes shone. "Phillip, you play with me."

"No, thanks, I'm not one for games," Phillip replied, his words pointed and aimed in Emily's direction.

The light went out in Carmie's eyes and Nick rushed to salve her disappointment. "I can fit in a game if you like, then you can help me unload the firewood. But I want the red piece. It's faster."

"No, it's not. I beat you last time." Carmie pushed her chair back from the table, but in her haste, it fell to the floor with a bang.

Phillip jumped. "Be careful," he admonished, his tone sharp.

Emily froze, her scone halfway to her mouth.

"It's okay. I'll pick it up," Carmie said, her movements clumsy.

Nick could have hugged her. Heaven help the man if he treated Carmie with disrespect. He liked that about Emily. She was indeed a mama-bear when it came to her sister. If Phillip couldn't see that, if he didn't realise the danger in his impatience, he'd be well on his way before the day was done.

"I took the liberty of making a dinner reservation at a winery in the Yarra Valley," Phillip went on. "It's only half an hour or so away by chopper."

Nick threw the die and watched from afar. He noticed Phillip's hand move to his trouser pocket and observed a square ridge. Did he plan to propose? Every hair on Nick's body rose and fell, and his stomach felt like someone had thrown a punch into the soft flesh. Phillip didn't love Emily. He didn't even know her. This was about ego. He was enamoured by how she looked beside him, how she fitted into his expensive, shallow life. Nick's gut twisted like someone had delved inside him and gripped his organs. It was like looking into a mirror. Had he been that shallow? Had his feelings for Charliese been little more than an ego trip? The thought snagged and stuck. Was that why she'd strayed?

Maybe Emily wanted a father-figure. He knew enough about her childhood to know her father had abandoned them at an early age. Perhaps there was some appeal to an older man who had money to spoil her.

"Nick, your turn."

Carmie's voice dragged him back to the board game in front of him. "You're beating me again," he play-growled.

"I know," she answered gaily. "You need more practice."

Nick tried to keep his attention on the game, but his ears strained to keep up with the conversation.

"I'm sorry. I can't leave Carmie tonight. Or Mum."

"Nick looks pretty at home here. Maybe he could come over and babysit?" Phillip's tone was petulant.

Nick was relieved to see Emily sit up straighter, her hand curled into a fist. "Thank you, but I'd rather be here. I don't want to go out. You're welcome to join us for dinner though."

"I had something special in mind."

Nick hadn't realised a man could pout. Apparently, when you're wealthy enough to get about in a helicopter, you're wealthy enough to pout.

"Again, I thank you for the kind thought."

Emily reached out to touch Phillip's hand and Nick was surprised by the electric reaction that sparked through his own body.

"Yes!" Carmen slipped up a ladder to the top row.

Nick readied to throw the die with renewed determination. His face was damaged goods, but he was a damn sight better man than Phillip. Even a week ago, he wouldn't have seen past his self-loathing. Now, he saw what Phillip couldn't. Nick had been that man. He'd been like Phillip. Oblivious to his own faults. Self-centred and narcissistic. Now, he understood why Charliese had decided to cut her losses. He wasn't that man anymore and for the first time in two years, the accident seemed more like a blessing and less like a disaster.

Emily stepped into the woodshed in time to see Nick ferrying the last load of wood towards the neat stack. His black t-shirt stretched tight across his muscular chest and his biceps bulged with the weight of the load. Emily fanned herself and blamed her light-headedness on the change of temperature after the warmth of the kitchen.

"That's it. Done." Carmie's cheerful tone rang across the chilly space.

"Thanks for your help, gorgeous girl. Great job."

"You have to stay for lunch *and* for dinner."

Please, don't, Emily thought, but Carmie's enthusiasm was hard to crush. "Yes. You're welcome to stay," she added, giving her presence away.

Nick spun around, his eyes brightening when he saw her, and his grin widened. She ignored the flush of warmth to her cheeks. What woman didn't like the flare of appreciation in a man's eyes? And this man? She wasn't sure whether to be thankful or angry regarding his kindness towards Carmie. His casual camaraderie appeared genuine, but Carmie's adoration was clear to see and if he hurt her, if he let her down, if he betrayed her in any way, Emily would google *best ways to kill a man without getting caught* and there'd be no hesitation.

"Thanks, I'd like that…"

His gaze ran over her, like a caress or a feather on bare skin.

"…but I don't want to cramp your style. You'd probably like some time to reconnect with Phillip."

"No, thank you. Phillip and I are friends and colleagues. We had a few unofficial dates, but I was very clear regarding my disinterest in a more serious relationship."

"You're very pragmatic."

"A girl has to protect herself."

"A girl could end up alone."

"Sometimes a girl would rather be alone than disappointed." Disappointed sounded so benign compared with the echo of long-ago injury and the pain that lingered still… the pain of not being worth the effort. She'd loved her father deeply, but he'd thrown her aside, because he didn't love her enough to deal with Carmie's genetic abnormality, which was hardly Carmie's fault. Emily wrapped her arms around her body as if she could shield herself in arrears. Or maybe it was to hold in the pain so Nick wouldn't see the tracts of it on her face.

There weren't too many men who treated Carmie with respect, but Carmie was vulnerable. She didn't understand other people's selfish motives. She didn't appreciate that a man might tell a girl what she wanted to hear, not because he meant it, but because he wanted to get into her panties. Not because he cared about her, but because he wanted to feed his ego and score with a beautiful woman. Emily had learned *that* the hard way and her IQ was nearly twice that of her sister's. Men couldn't be trusted. Men sensed vulnerability like crows sensed roadkill.

She stood with her feet apart and strove for a warrior-princess glare, but Nick's gaze captured hers and the intensity of it left her weak at her warrior-princess knees.

"Sometimes a man would rather be alone than to disappoint."

His gaze was like a laser beam. Something shifted inside her, cracked and broke free as she recognised his pain. So, he knew. He understood. A part of her was in freefall, like a feather on a draught of hot air. A part of her—that part used to being alone—lifted its crying head, wiped its tears and connected with the man across the woodshed.

"What's for dessert?" Carmie's voice was loud in the thick silence.

"Apple pie."

"Yay!" Carmie danced into her line of vision and wrapped her arms around Emily's waist. Emily leaned forward to kiss Carmie's hair, the sweet fruity scent of it a comforting buoy in a churning sea.

"Where's your guest?"

"He headed over to the cottage to get settled." Where he'd sleep. *Alone.* Emily had been right to chop him at their unofficial fifth date. She'd seen his distaste for Carmie. His impatience. His intolerance. She didn't want him here, but she owed him the opportunity to see for himself why it would never have worked between them. His family was wealthy and moved in social circles she didn't. He'd soon realise and appreciate the out she'd offered him.

"Shall we head in? I could do with a hot chocolate. What about you, Carmie? We've been working hard." Nick reached for his jumper and pulled it on.

Emily grieved the visual loss. She linked hands with Carmie, and they walked together towards the house.

"Hot chocolate! Yes, Nick. What a good idea! You're very smart."

"Not nearly as smart as your sister."

Emily eyed him over Carmie's head. What did he mean by that? And then it struck her. He was glad she didn't want Phillip here. Why? Was he jealous? No. That made no sense. There was nothing between them but old animosity, old scars, and old secrets. He hadn't even bothered to drop in over the past week, but then she recalled what he'd said. That a man would rather be alone than to disappoint. And his reaction last weekend when her gaze had shifted to the damaged side of his face. Did he think his looks were a disappointment? Of course, he must. But he didn't know her at all if he thought she was the kind of person who judged someone by their appearance. She'd long ago learned that perfection was no better than imperfection. Not that she cared one way or the other. Her negative opinion of him was rooted in something far deeper than the way he looked, although Charliese's tirade about him didn't fit with the man she'd seen so far. Not the man who played snakes and ladders with Carmie. Not the man who cared enough about her sister to bring her flowers because they were her favourite and grew in his garden. Not the man who cooked meals for his neighbours because they were in need. The thoughts were like barbed wire, catching and ripping at the fabric of her memories.

She stepped onto the veranda and wriggled out of her boots, moving into the house in her thick socks. Nick helped Carmie loosen hers and caught Emily's gaze. Connection zapped between them, leaving her breathless and a tad light-headed. Oh, no. That couldn't happen. She couldn't soften towards

Nick. That wasn't an option. She twisted the ring on her finger and remembered Charliese's warning. Better alone than gone like her friend or broken like her mum. Better alone and strong than in love and weak.

"We're back," she called out. She'd left her mum sitting by the fire with a mug of hot soup, but as soon as she rounded the corner, she saw the chair was empty. She turned to Nick and Carmie. "I need to check on Mum. Then I'll make us hot chocolate."

Her eyes took a moment to adjust to the darkness in her mum's room, but she saw her pull the bedclothes higher, so she hadn't fallen asleep yet. "Hi, Mum. Are you feeling okay?"

"I'm done in, love, but thanks for the soup." Her mum's voice was muffled by the bedding.

"I'll wake you in time for dinner. Nick and Phillip are joining us."

"Phillip seems like a nice man."

"Yes, he does, doesn't he? Have a good sleep, Mum." Phillip did seem like a nice man, but even a nice man lost interest when he realised a woman came with a disabled sister and a child-mum, for good measure. At that point, in her experience, most men found the deal not so sweet. In fact, it became downright bitter. Well, thank you, universe, because without her family, she would have been suckered in by the likes of Phillip.

Emily entered the kitchen. There was the scent of freshly baked bread from the machine on the bench and a wave of garlicky goodness from the huge pot of pumpkin and lentil soup on the stove. Her stomach growled in response. She stalled when she saw Nick and Carmie at the bench, stirring a saucepan of steaming milk. Carmie broke into peals of laughter as she added another marshmallow to each mug.

"We made the hot chocolate," Carmie said. "With marshmallows. Lots of them."

"You're a gun in the kitchen, Wheatley."

"Not *just* in the kitchen." He poured hot milk into each of the mugs and gave them a stir.

A blast of desire hit Emily square in the midriff and fanned out in all directions. Whoa. He didn't pull any punches when he came on to a woman and if she wasn't mistaken, he'd just come on to her. "I guess you're pretty handy with an axe, too. Thanks for the firewood."

"You're welcome." He sipped his hot chocolate and wiggled his foamy moustache at Carmie who laughed until she got the hiccups.

Emily couldn't help smiling. There was a lot to like about a man who could make fun of himself. Not that she was looking for a man. Especially not *this* man.

"I'll need to head home after lunch and have a shower. What time did you have in mind for dinner tonight?"

Another blast detonated as a vision of him naked under pelting water appeared in her mind's eye. Where was his anger and scorn? She preferred his judgemental wrath to the heat that seemed to radiate off him, drawing her in with its seductive warmth.

"Seven would be good. I hope you like roast lamb."

"You sure know the way to a man's heart." His tone was jocular, but there was nothing funny about the intensity of his gaze.

"The pumpkin soup's ready, but we'll wait for Phillip to join us."

"With freshly baked bread?" He took a deep breath and closed his eyes. "You're killing me."

If it only took a loaf of fresh bread to finish him off, then she wouldn't need to google other options. She'd just load up the bread machine and be done. Goal achieved. "Yes, and it's nearly ready."

"Can I show Nick the new hens? Come on, Joey." Carmie prodded him out of his pouch, and he flicked his ears, leaning against her.

"Hens, huh? I hope you put them in at night."

"Yes, silly. Or a fox will eat them. Their names are Happy... Sleepy... Dopey... Em, what are the rest?"

"Bashful, Sneezy, Grumpy and Doc. We named Grumpy after you," Emily said with a laugh.

"I bet she's the good-looking one."

"She is," Carmie said, her tone incredulous. "And come see the vegie garden. We planted lettuce and spinach and carrots... and what else, Em?"

"Leek, peas and spring onion. We valiantly fought the weeds and the hens were pretty happy with the spoils."

Nick reached over and took Emily's hands in his. His calloused skin was a warm abrasion against hers, his touch like a brand. Her senses seized. Her breath stopped. Her ears roared. His blue, blue gaze drew her like a magnet and heat rushed to her cheeks.

"Just checking for blisters and broken nails, but it looks like you made it out okay."

"Check mine!" Carmie pulled his hands away. "Check mine, Nick."

Nick inspected her hands, his gaze steady on her bitten nails and soft palms. Emily observed the rush of pink to her sister's cheeks and knew exactly how she felt. How had she relaxed her guard for even a moment? There was nowhere this could go. Nowhere. But, tell that to the part of her soul that had woken and waited. For what, Emily wasn't even sure. She turned her attention back to the soup.

Phillip's voice called from the hallway. "Where is everyone?"

"In here," she called and her heart plummeted in her chest. He was a reminder of everything she'd risked coming home. A reminder of the glamour and the shine and the fairy-tale fun of her job. She liked designer clothes. She liked being admired. She liked the attention that came with being beautiful, but she knew it wasn't real. She needed this. She needed her visits home to stay grounded. To stay sane. To keep it together.

Phillip, on the other hand, had no idea. He was so enmeshed in his own fake-power, he'd lost perspective. He didn't like to be told no. He didn't like to lose. He didn't like to be reminded that not everyone was perfect. His world was candlelit dinners and tropical paradises, but none of it was real. It was an illusion. A lovely, tempting, fickle illusion.

"How about a walk after lunch. I'd like to wander these country lanes with my favourite girl and take in the scenery. I hear there are a lot of koalas about."

"That's a nice idea." Emily forced herself to smile and turned her attention to Carmie. "Lunch is nearly ready so if you want to show Nick the hens, you'd better get going."

Carmie grabbed Nick by the hand. "We're off."

"Wait. Take the scraps with you." Emily reached for the small bucket of vegetable scraps that sat on the bench. "They'll enjoy these."

"Will there be eggs, Em?"

"Not yet. They're too young, but soon." The buzzer went off on the bread machine and she flicked the top up. The crust was perfectly golden.

"Five minutes," Nick promised, and disappeared behind Carmie and Joey.

"It's not hygienic to have a baby kangaroo in the kitchen." Phillip strode towards her and leaned against the bench.

"You're probably right, but he can't go out in the cold. He's too young. Besides, he still has formula twice a day."

"Who are you and where is the Emily Stone I know and love?"

"I'd like to say she's here, but I'm not sure she's real, which is why I'm not interested in a more serious relationship." The muscles in Emily's neck tightened and balled and she dug her nails into the knot.

"I want to whisk you away and treat you the way you deserve to be treated."

He drew her into his arms, and she fought the rigidity in her limbs. Two weeks ago, she would have melted against him, but now she pulled away, disguising her reaction with movement. She picked up the kettle and turned on the tap. "Would you like a tea?" She gazed out of the window, past the green of the pasture, to where the clouds gathered, black and heavy and swollen on the horizon. Rain fell somewhere distant, in misty sheets highlighted by the sun.

"That would be lovely, my dear. Thank you." He settled himself against the island bench. "I'm sure you'll find another carer for your family. It's madness to leave your career right now when it's going so well. You know how difficult it is to gain momentum. If you step back for too long, another beautiful girl will step up and take your place. It's not like there's any shortage."

"I know." The muscles across her shoulders tensed and banded. She dug her fingertips into the burning centre and kneaded the knots, shocked to find Phillip had come up close behind her.

"Here, let me help."

His touch was hot and rhythmic, but a part of her was in flight mode, all tangled and tight.

"Let me look after you," he soothed. "Let me spoil you. Let me please you. Let me take you back to where you belong."

"This is where I belong. Here. This is why we can't be more than friends. I'm sorry." She stepped away and wrapped her arms around her body.

"I understand your need to look after your family. I couldn't admire you more. You're amazing. You're such a supportive sister and daughter, but you're a grown woman. You need to live your own life. Your sister needs to live *her* own life."

"My sister can't live her own life. She can't look after herself. She's not independent and she never will be." Emily's hands curled into fists, her nails digging into her palms. "She needs me, and I will always be there for her. Don't you see? I'm not the person you think I am. I'm not free to create the life you have in mind, which is why I made it easy for both of us. I need to be here for my sister. For my mum. We're a package deal and any man I date needs to know that."

"I can't see any man accepting those terms." His tone was dull and flat and final.

"Nor can I." Emily turned away and reached for the kettle. Her grip was tight enough to bare her knuckles.

"Not all men are so block-stupid." Nick's voice came from the doorway.

Emily turned towards him. "All men from my experience. Where's Carmie?"

"She went to the bathroom."

67

"Thank goodness. How much did you hear?"

"Enough." His gaze burned into hers. Blue fire. Blue ice.

A part of her near shattered and she called on all of her warrior princess strength. She didn't need a man. She didn't want a man. She was better off alone. "I'll serve up." She poured water into the kettle and flicked the switch with a little more force than was necessary. She turned her attention to lunch and scooped soup into bowls, sprinkling chopped chives on top. When she turned with a bowl in each hand, she found the two men a short distance apart, their feet wide, their eyes boring into each other with silent contempt. Emily couldn't care less about either one of them. She lowered the bowls to the table and turned to get the bread.

The meal would have been a silent affair had it not been for Carmie's delightful chatter. Emily loved her sister, and, in truth, it was no hardship to look after her. The hardship came in the guise of the men who pretended to care. The men who wouldn't know love if it stepped up and saluted them. Thanks to Carmie, Emily was immune to them. Thanks to Carmie, she wasn't looking for a long-term proposition. Thanks to Carmie, she knew better than to think a man would ever love her, the real her, the person inside the pretty package.

Chapter Four

Phillip reached for her hand and Emily didn't have the heart to shun him. Not when she had the smallest of hopes he might have it in his heart to understand and support her. He'd cared enough to come here.

The sun shone through the gaps in the burgeoning black clouds and with the warmth of it on her back and the quiet scenery around her, she strove to relax. But the air was tight and fraught with the storm that brewed, the sky a thickening mass of black and every kind of grey, a seething powerhouse of energy.

"Look." She pointed to a scraggly gum by the side of the road. "Do you see him?" A koala snuggled in the crook of the branch, its eyes scrunched closed, its head tucked into its tummy, its back soaking up the sun.

"Where?"

Phillip drew her close and settled his face against hers as he looked where she pointed. He was warm, and his touch stirred the feelings she didn't want to feel for him. Okay, she might have liked him and there may have been a strong attraction between them, but it wasn't real.

"I see it." His head turned, and he pressed his forehead against hers. "I have feelings for you, my dear. I want to make you happy. I want you in my life…"

"I appreciate that very much." It would be easy to fall into his familiar warmth, but she wasn't in love with him. A part of her wanted the fairy tale. But even in fairy tales, things weren't as they seemed. The carriage was a pumpkin. The footmen were mice. The ball gown, just rags. "But whatever this is between us, it won't work. I am sorry." Her skin tightened. Her heart clenched. Her temple throbbed.

"Your life is more complicated than I realised."

Emily stepped back and her gaze connected with his. "Yes, it is." She turned away from him and they started walking. The walk had been a good idea. The fresh air, the rolling paddocks, the gorgeous vista all around them. The heavy threat of rain and tempest. She was happy here. She'd been happy here as a child. It was a beautiful place. Quiet. Isolated. Wild. She didn't need the lights, the fast-paced travel, the glamour.

Besides, she and Carmie could travel.

And draw attention? Her gut knotted. People tended to stare at them, but she'd learned to be tough. To ignore them. To let their questions and judgement roll over her.

Emily dug her hands into her pockets, and they walked in silence. The air was cold, and the wind pulled at them, whipping her ponytail to the side. The sun filtered through the clouds in rays, one part of the landscape basking in the sun, another in dark shadow. A herd of black cattle grazed in the paddock to their left—Nick's property. The sound of a calf broke the quiet, its throaty bellow pulsing like a siren. Their heads lifted as she and Phillip drew near, and disturbed, they lumbered away in the opposite direction, their big bodies slow to gain momentum. There was the strong scent of manure and freshly turned earth from the clods lifted by their feet.

The view stretched before them. The green expanse of the land. The steely grey of the bay, spattered with white caps. The sky, bruised and bloated with blacks and greys and purple.

It was eerily quiet, like the birds had hunkered down. Like the land held its breath.

There was the sound of their steps on the tiny stones of the corrugated road. And the distressed call of a calf. The answering bellow of its mum. More urgent now.

The sound pulled at her. Was something wrong? The thought jolted her from the companionable silence. "I hope that calf's alright."

"You worry about everyone else, but who worries about you?" He wrapped his arm around her, drawing her close.

"I'm fine, Phillip. I've been alone for a very long time."

"I have a better understanding of that now. I'm sorry you felt you couldn't trust me with the truth. I thought we were friends."

"I'm sorry to disappoint you." To be disappointed by you. The thought was unfair. He'd been nice enough to follow her and to make sure she was okay. Perhaps she and Phillip would remain friends. "Thank you for understanding. I hope you can forgive me."

"There's nothing to forgive." He was quiet for a long moment. "I hope you find someone to take care of your mum and sister soon. We need you back at work."

"I know. You're right." The sun disappeared behind the clouds and the temperature seemed to drop several degrees. Emily pulled the zip higher on the front of her puffer jacket. "Shall we head back?"

The calf bellowed again. A sharp, deep-throated cry that went on and on, joined by the alarmed cry of its mum. Emily's skin prickled with alarm. "Something's wrong. We need to check that out." It was one of Nick's animals.

"I don't know anything about cattle and we're not going in there with them. It's not safe. They're huge. What if they stampede? No, Emily. I don't think it's a good idea."

"I can't leave the poor thing. Listen to it. There's something very wrong." Emily used her foot and hand to create an opening in the barbed wire fence. "You go first."

"I'm not going in there."

"Then hold it for me so I can go in." Emily eyed the fence. There was no chance she could roll under it without getting her puffer jacket caught in the barbs. She could climb over at the post if she had to, but it would be easier to slip through the gap. "Press your foot down on the wire and lift the top one with your hands."

Phillip did as she asked, but she could tell from his expression that he wasn't happy about it.

"Thanks. Could you ask mum to call Nick? It's his property." She took off in a full run towards the sound, which came in staccato beats, then silence. It was getting tired. Oh, she hoped she wasn't too late. There, in the dam. In the water. She spun back. "Phillip," she yelled. "Get Nick. Tell him it's urgent. Hurry."

"I can't leave you."

"You have to. I didn't bring my phone. Run."

The calf was caught in the mud and the more it struggled, the deeper it sank into the gluey mess. Its mother roamed the perimeter, her calls as anxious as the calf's, which were getting weak. Emily picked up a solid branch and carried it to defend herself. The last thing she needed was an irate, out-of-her-mind-with-hysteria, mama-beast taking her worries out on her. What could she do? The calf's head disappeared under the muddy swirl of the water, came up again. Hell, there wasn't time to think. She stepped into the quagmire, her own feet sinking. The mud sucked at them and she struggled to pull them out again.

She threw the branch down, stepped onto it and gained some traction. She grabbed at the calf's head and forced her knee under its neck, making soothing sounds. There was no way she could get it out. How long could she hold it? *Hurry, Phillip. Come on, Nick.*

Every time the calf struggled, it took them both deeper into the muck.

If it wasn't for the branch, she, too, would have lost her grip. She was up to her waist, now. She tried to count. Tried to stop the panic that grabbed at her as surely as the mud. Tried to assess the passing time. Her body shook. Her bones felt stiff like rigor mortis had set in. Her teeth chattered together, but she held on. The calf collapsed against her, exhausted. The whites of its eyes flashed. Its nostrils flared. Its breath came in sharp staccatos. Would it die of fright? Would its weight drag her under? Her hands were numb. Her feet cold to the point of pain. How much longer?

And then she heard it. The sound of a tractor in the distance. She reassured the calf and the storming mother, who paced back and forth on the bank, her hooves digging up the soft soil. "It's going to be okay, little one. Nick will come. Hold on." *Hold on*, she repeated for herself, and she held on by sheer grit, by sheer force of will. And she stayed as still as she could. The calf's writhing movement forced them deeper into the muck. She clung to its wet, muddy coat. It was exhausted, and without her support, it would have given up and gone under.

Emily held on. Held on and counted. And when she thought she couldn't hold on for another moment, when the muscles in her back moved past a scream to a dull roar in her ears, when her mind started to despair, the distant throb of the tractor became a loud, guttural roar and Nick thundered down the slope towards her, the sky black behind him, the wind picking up and fanning through the grass. He turned the tractor at the last moment so the back of it faced her. He planned to drag them out with the tractor? Of course. There was no other way to pull them out against the suction of the mud.

He was off the tractor before it stopped moving. He attached a rope to the back, unravelling it towards her. He tied a loop in the end and threw it to her. "Can you get it around the calf's head? And under its front legs?

Speech was near past her. Like the mud, exhaustion pulled at her. She shook her head. "Can't let go."

Nick splashed into the mud and grappled to get the rope around the calf's neck, his gaze on hers, his eyes bright with fear, raw, unadulterated fear.

"Is it safe?" The words took every last skerrick of her energy. Emily couldn't move. They had no choice. The calf's legs were stuck in the mud. Its belly. Its tail.

Nick soothed her with noises very like the ones she'd made for the calf. His forehead puckered with concentration. His chin was determined. His jaw, tight. Panic became a deafening rattle in her ears or maybe that was her teeth. She was cold. So. Cold. Nick struggled to get out of the mud, the water swirling around his legs. He held onto the rope and pulled himself out. "Do you know how to drive a tractor?"

She shook her head. "I'm stuck, too." She pulled at one foot, but the mud was like wet concrete and the movement made her sink deeper, almost up to her chest and panic gripped her like a fist around her throat.

"Hold onto the rope. Wrap your arm around the calf."

Emily slid her arm under the rope where it circled the calf's neck. She could protect its throat, but how the hell was this going to work? Nick staggered towards the tractor and climbed into the cab. He shoved it into gear, and it moved, its giant tread spitting wads of soft earth into the air. The rope pulled tight and Emily coaxed the calf to fight. "Come on, little one. We've got this. You've got this." Its eyes rolled in its head and its cry was desperate as the tug of the tractor fought the suction of the mud and drew them slowly, slowly towards the bank. Emily fought to keep the calf's head above the water, its flaring nostrils up and out of the muck. Both of them fought the mud. Nick yelled, but Emily's focus was on keeping her own head above the water. The extrication was slow, but as the calf's weight was taken from its legs, it began to kick out and the grip of the mud loosened. When it scrabbled to stand, Emily called to Nick to stop. Just when she thought they were safe, her grip on the rope slipped and her feet lost traction. She fell backwards, the weight of her wet puffer pulling her down into the muddy arms of the water. She struggled against it, pushing up but hit mud. Her lungs screamed. She thrashed and fought the clutch of it, but her head spun, her mind reeled. And then there was light. There was air. Her lungs grabbed at it, snatching breath like it might be taken away again. And there was Nick's face, a mask of horror, his eyes glazed with fear, his hands strong around her waist. He pulled her close, seemingly frozen, paralysed.

"Get us out of here, Wheatley." Her voice came to her ears from an eery distance. It seemed to snap him out of whatever had gripped him, and he dragged her, half falling towards the bank, pulling on the rope, his muscles hard and solid against her.

When she was safe, their eyes connected for a moment, a brief moment in truth, but long enough for him to share his fear, his worry, his relief. And she got it. She could have drowned. Like Charliese. He'd have had her death on his conscience, too. She'd made him relive that horror. Emily collapsed against the bank. Every muscle screamed and trembled. Her feet howled with the cold. Her body convulsed with it. She could have died, unable to extricate herself from the mud. Her breath came in pants. Short and sharp.

"Don't move."

There was no risk of that. She couldn't have moved if she'd tried. Her body was like jelly. Quivery and not quite solid. She dropped her head on her arms, conscious of the firm earth beneath her, the strong skitter of her heartbeat inside her chest.

Nick pulled away to deal with the calf. To drag it further from the muck. Exhausted, its head lolled to the muddy ground. Its mother hovered nearby, bawling, an anxious sound that sawed the air.

It wasn't safe yet.

Nick raced for towels and blankets and wrapped a couple tightly around Emily. "Here. You need to get warm." He dried the calf with a towel, massaging its muscles, and rubbing it all over. He tucked blankets around it and headed back to the tractor, pulling out a thermos of coffee.

Emily watched his hands shake, wet and cold, as he poured a small amount into the steel cup, sloshing some over the side. He slid a hip flask from his pocket and put a shot of something into it. Her body recoiled, frozen as it was, and her thoughts flew back to the alcohol-soaked man she'd met on the ferry a little over a week ago.

"Here."

Emily reached for it, but her hands shook too much to hold it.

"Wait."

Nick's lips were blue, his teeth banging together as he held it up to her mouth and she breathed in the rich aroma, laced with whiskey. She sipped, and the steamy warmth created a rosy glow inside her. She wrapped her hands around the cup and with her full concentration, she was able to take hold, though it splashed onto the ground.

"Thank. You."

Nick crouched in front of her, his gaze hypnotising. "You keep surprising me, Emily Stone." Lightning flashed behind him, a vivid arc against the ominous blackness.

She nodded, for what could she say, but warmth spread through her. The kind of warmth that radiated from the inside out. She liked that look on his face. She liked surprising him in a good way. She liked it when he saw past the pretty to the person inside and didn't mind what he saw.

"The calf needs a shot of whiskey too—medicinal—but that storm's not going to wait forever." Thunder rumbled around them, shaking the ground.

The mother hovered close by, her nose nudging her calf. He wasn't up to standing yet. He was done in. Exhausted. The whiskey helped revive him, but he needed to stand to take a drink from his mum. The cow nudged him again. "Come on, mate." Nick helped pull his front feet out from beneath him, but the calf wasn't ready to stand. He shook with the cold or the fright or both. He rested his head in Nick's wet lap and closed his eyes.

"Will he live?"

"I'm not sure, but his chances are a damn sight better out here than they were in there. You saved his life. He was done in."

"He was."

"I've installed water troughs in all of the paddocks to avoid this. The plumbing's nearly done. The last time this happened, it wasn't such a bright outcome. He's not the first animal to get caught."

Emily looked out across the paddocks. It was dark, the sun blotted out by the clouds that hung black and bruised, violet roiling all the way to the horizon. The air was eerily still. "There's a hell of a storm coming."

"There is. We need to get this little guy up to the trees where it's more sheltered and protected. Then we need to get you home."

"I'm okay, now. Warmer. How will we move him?" The calf's mother stood nearby, her body tense and ready to flee, her ears flicking, her tail swishing from one side to the other. She wanted her baby back and she wasn't leaving without him.

"We'll wait a bit longer. I'm hoping he'll stand. He needs a drink from his mum."

"How do you do this alone?"

"The farm? With great difficulty. I hire in help when I need it. I have a dog. A kelpie, but he's still learning the ropes and times like these, he makes it worse."

Emily surveyed the undulating hills and the sea beyond. "This farm used to belong to my grandparents. A long time ago. Before your parents bought it." She felt connected to the earth beneath her, like the roots of her own soul went deep into its rich loamy soil. "I thought you'd want to leave here after your mum passed, but I understand now." She'd seen it in his face. The fear. The worry. The relief when the calf was safe. If she'd learned nothing else about him over the past week, she'd learned that. He loved his farm. Her walks told her that. His fences were straight. No bracken or blackberry bushes like some of the farms. No cake-weed in his pasture. His animals were shiny and solid and well cared for. None of it made sense. He wasn't the man Charliese had described and he wasn't the drunk she'd assumed him to be. No alcoholic cared for anyone or anything except for themselves and their booze.

"That's something I didn't know," he said, his gaze holding hers while he stroked the calf's neck. "My dad loved this place. He was a decent man. A good father, but when I was younger, I couldn't wait to leave." His gaze settled on the horizon. "When he died ten years ago, I was busy overseas, seeking fame. Everything deteriorated here and fell into disrepair. The fences. The pasture. Mum couldn't manage by herself. I should have come home sooner."

Emily sipped her coffee, swallowing against the well of emotion that rose in her throat, bottomless and fathoms deep. She tightened the blanket around her—cold, so cold—her voice jerky. "You were an amazing success. He would have been proud of you. Most of us couldn't wait to leave."

They were silent for a long moment and she savoured the rich scent of the coffee, cuddling the cup close. Her lips quivered and her shoulders hunched under the blanket. "My father couldn't wait to leave." Her gaze moved away. Across the grass and the muck. Across the dam water that mirrored the seething mass of clouds above, giving it the appearance of life. There was a massive rift in the mud where they'd dragged the calf out and there were deep holes where hooves and feet had sunk in. Her body shook. From the cold. From the anger that stormed inside her. "He couldn't handle Carmie's disability. She embarrassed him."

Shadows stirred in the depths of Nick's blue gaze. "But he left you, too. And you did nothing to embarrass him."

"True." Emily blamed the pain in her chest, and the sharp push and pull of her emotions on her near brush with death. Air made it into her lungs, but it had nowhere to go. Her heart was paralysed. Like it couldn't pump blood. Like it hurt too much to breathe. Her head spun. Her vision darkened. Black spots danced before her eyes.

"Are you okay?"

Nick's voice came from a distance. A long, eerie echoey distance...

Emily was slow to gather her senses. There was a tender, rhythmic stroke against her head, the icy breath of the wind against her forehead, a shivery jitteriness in her limbs. She opened her eyes and found herself in Nick's lap, his worried blue gaze steady on hers. She should have panicked and moved away, but her first reaction was to settle and calm and stay. He stroked her hair, his expression one of warmth and care.

"Welcome back, soldier. You fainted."

"I did? I've never fainted before."

"You pushed yourself too hard, Em. You were done in."

"I had to. He would have gone under. He would have died."

"Yep. You saved his life and risked your own."

She struggled to sit up. "Is he okay?"

"Relax. Stay. He's fine." Nick's tone was like a warm wrap or melted marshmallow, and it softened the hard edges inside her. "He's up, having a drink from his mum."

"He is? Oh, that's good." Emily closed her eyes and allowed herself to float with the bewitching stroke of his hands. His touch stirred her—deeply—and her mind couldn't get a grip. Her body relaxed into the soft earth, her thoughts spinning, her lips trembling with the cold.

"That's better than good. You saved his life. You're still shivering."

Nick drew her into his arms—his strong, capable arms—and pulled her blanket-clad body against his firm, muscular chest and into his lap. She should have fought it, but she had no fight left. She curled up against him and he held her close. Her body warmed and heated. She fitted against him like they'd been made for each other. His grip was tight, and she felt comforted, like he knew her soul ached. Like he knew how deeply she hurt. He kissed her on the forehead and the touch of his lips ignited something inside her that spun and rocketed like a firework into the black, black sky. Desire. It spread through her like a rogue flame, the flare of heat, the flash of light, the fanning front devouring the forest of thorns around her heart.

His face lowered to hers, the soft plumpness of his lips, the raw intensity of his eyes, the blade of his nose a nanometre from hers. Emily reached out to touch his ravaged cheek, her hand travelling over the puckered skin, the fiery redness. His eyes flashed with desolation, his soul desperate and exposed, his distaste for himself clear to see. But the more he resisted, the deeper she sank. The more he fought what pulsed between them like it lived and breathed, the more she surrendered. The more he second-guessed himself, the more she wanted.

But Charliese was wedged between them like an impassable wall.

"Tell me about the accident." Emily had hated Nick for his

crap driving, his selfish survival, and his careless disregard for the woman he'd married. The whole damn mess. She had the newspaper clippings still. The shrieking headlines about the Hollywood movie star, disfigured for life, and the death of his wife.

Nick's eyes glazed with memories and Emily could see the edges, the icy bite, the shadows, bruised and battered, in the blue of his eyes. Her heart sank like she'd ventured too far into the muddy quicksand of the dam. She didn't want to feel for him. She didn't want to understand his side of the story. She was glad he'd suffered. Or at least, she had been, until she'd gotten to know the man he'd become. The pain of his suffering was there in his eyes. His gaze held hers like he wanted to share, like he wanted to pull free, but was so deeply submerged he needed something stronger than a Massey Ferguson to pull him out.

A wave of compassion overwhelmed her, and she brushed her lips—trembling, but not from the cold—against the warmth of his. She pulled back—not far—enough to seek what stormed in his eyes. His gaze was bleak like he had nothing to give. Like a murder of crows had stripped the flesh from his bones. Tears sprang to Emily's eyes and her chest hurt like someone had taken her own heart and wrung every last drop of blood from it. It contracted and squeezed, until the tightness hindered her breath. It hurt for the terrible thing that had happened to him, the terrible thing that had happened to her friend.

"I don't like to talk about it."

Lightning flashed and his face, distorted with all he held in, was imprinted in her memory. A man burdened with grief. A man whose self-loathing was worse than any punishment she could have wished upon him. And that icy corner of her heart that sought vengeance for Charliese heated and thawed.

"Besides, you have problems of your own. You don't need to listen to mine."

"A problem shared is a problem halved. You supported me. You helped my family. You saved my life. I want to be there for you, too." And she did. Her words were underscored by a deep roll of thunder that growled and prowled and roiled in the thick black of the sky.

"You saved my livestock." Her attention returned to the calf and joy flashed through her. He pulled and sucked and drank from his mum, his muddy bottom thrust to the sky, his tail flicking, his front legs folded. His mum nuzzled him with her nose and she cleaned his coat with her long tongue.

"I couldn't bear not to help. I didn't have a choice." Lightning cracked in the air.

"You're a good person. Compassionate. Your values are in the right place and I'm sorry that surprised me. I thought..."

"I was like Phillip? Self-centred, self-obsessed, and self-serving."

"Yes."

"I see him, Nick, I know what he is. But he treats me like a queen."

"Is that what you need? To be treated like a queen?" She heard the desolation in his question. The wounded man. The humble man.

"No, but it was nice for a while."

"How long did you date him?" His gaze held hers, raw and clear.

"Five unofficial dates." She didn't need to think. Her response was quick. Automatic.

"Five dates exactly?"

"Any more than that and it gets complicated. I don't invite men home, and I find that after five dates, reality starts to ruin the fantasy."

"Because of Carmie?"

"Looking beautiful only gets a girl so far and in my experience, men want the fantasy, not the reality. I'd rather leave on my terms than be left and there are few men—none—in my experience who can handle the nature of my obligations. I love Carmie. I want to be there for her. I don't expect a man to understand that or to be there for me."

It was like something cosmic had sucked the oxygen from the air or the world held its breath. The atmosphere was still and eerily swollen.

Nick's gaze shot to the horizon and she could see the worry, the awareness, like he, too, felt the ominous clutch of the air. But he turned his attention back to her, his forehead scrunched, his focus on her words. "I used to be like him."

"Who?"

"Phillip. Like the men you date. I married a beautiful woman because she made me feel good about myself. I was so full of my own ego that I was blind. I thought the accident ruined my life. Now I realise, it opened my eyes." He rocked and held her close, his gaze on the murky horizon. "On the day of the accident, not long before, Charliese told me she wanted a divorce. I was hurt. Angry. My mind wasn't on the road. The wheel hit a hole in the bitumen I think... there was a bang and we flipped through the air. It all happened so fast. There was a river. We hit the water before I could process what had happened. There was a tree... it gouged my face and ripped my scalp from the bone, but it saved my life. When the car went under, it held me against the force of the water. But Charliese was trapped and tangled under the water. It all happened so quickly. I tried to free her, but I couldn't get her out."

Emily reeled with the awful image he'd created. She felt the hard thud of his heart against her, the kerthump, kerthump, kerthump, like he'd run a marathon and fought for air.

"It was an accident." She'd blamed him. His crappy driving. His selfish survival. She'd thought he'd gotten off lightly compared with Charliese, but he'd suffered. He suffered still. He suffered every day.

"I was responsible. I was a despicable, self-centred jerk, who couldn't tolerate the ego-hit of a wife who wanted out. I don't blame her anymore. I drank too much. I was obsessed with my own career. The accident helped me to see what I hadn't seen before." He paused and the darkness that swirled around them swirled in his eyes. "She was afraid I'd leave her. She didn't trust me. She didn't trust me because I wasn't trustworthy."

"Your scar must remind you every time you look in a mirror." Her gaze lowered to the square line of his jaw and the dark stubble there. The good side of his face. The blue of his eyes flashed bright with the flickering electricity in the sky.

"I blamed her. I blamed everyone except myself. Now I realise I didn't deserve her. I didn't deserve the success that fell into my lap because of my good looks. God giveth and God taketh away." His tone was bitter like the words were unpalatable, but his gaze was raw. Desire was there, a flash of heat in a barren landscape, but so too was despair. He looked at her like she was everything he desired but didn't deserve.

Emily felt safe in his arms, bundled in a blankety cocoon. Her heart beat thick and fast. She breached the tiny distance between them and pressed her lips against the soft heat of his. Her body melted like she was made of wax and had been touched by flame. For a mind-spinning moment, he responded, and she allowed herself to fall into the tempting taste of a kiss that was more a meeting of souls than a meeting of mouths. For a body-churning second, she breathed him in and savoured his musky scent, the sweet spice of his aftershave. For an earth-shifting minute, she didn't resist and neither did he. She didn't listen to the words of warning that whispered in her head. She didn't fight the tide of feelings that connected her with the wound inside of the man. And the connection was strong, like she recognised a kindred spirit or the man of her dreams. The fantasy coloured her vision, making it rosy and pretty and possible.

It was the first splotches of cold rain upon her face that broke the spell. Splotches fast followed by more until the heavens opened and water poured on them like a bucket of ice from above, furiously charged by the wind that whirled around them like a whip.

Nick dragged her to her feet and Emily struggled to stand. Her gaze shifted to the mother and the calf, to the fractured water on the surface of the dam, anywhere but on the man beside her. "Look," she cried. The cow had used her nose to nudge the calf towards the trees and shelter, her long tongue licking him and near knocking him off his feet, but he managed to move.

"They're fine. We need to get out of this."

Nick wrapped his arms around her and pulled her towards the cab of the tractor. "You'll have to sit on my lap. It's a one-man show. My place is closer than yours. We need to get you warm and dry."

The cab was small and the single driver's seat filled the space. Rain pelted against the glass and the wipers struggled to clear it for long enough to see. Water poured from the sky like frozen tears, belting against the glass with the fury of the wind. The tractor slid in the soft earth and struggled to gain traction. Fear twisted its bony hands around Emily's throat and dug skeletal fingers into her mind. Would they slip back? Would they end up in the dam, trapped under the water? Like Charliese. Would she, too, suffocate and drown, unable to be saved?

Emily couldn't get the image of her friend out of her mind or the sensation of her own lungs screaming while she struggled against the mud and the weight of the water. Was it the seatbelt or the tree that had trapped Charliese in the car? Emily's heart pounded in her chest. Blood blasted through her veins, a loud kerthump in her ears and the tractor growled beneath her like a hulking beast. Thunder grumbled and roared from the roiling sky and the air throbbed. Lightning flashed, angry forks of electricity that arced and cracked like a horseman's whip and a nearby tree burst into flame.

Emily jumped, her body rigid. Would lightning strike them, too? Would the rubber tyres of the tractor be enough to protect them?

"It's fine. We'll be fine." Nick's voice was distant in the small space, difficult to hear against the slap of the rain and the whip of the wind. "The rain will deal with it."

Emily's limbs let go of the rigor mortis that glued them rigid. She was safe with Nick.

Charliese hadn't been safe with Nick.

The thought slammed into her brain like a wayward thorn and wedged there, a pointy reminder that she couldn't trust him. He wasn't trustworthy. He'd said so himself. Charliese hadn't trusted him.

And what about Carmie. She'd been so caught up in the

moment, like a precious, pearly bubble carved out of time, that she'd forgotten her sister's crush on Nick. A shiver returned to her lips, a chatter to her teeth. Her gaze steadied on the watery world beyond the glass. It felt as if the heavens cried along with her heart. The tractor slipped and lost traction, and she grabbed at Nick's arm and held on.

This couldn't happen. This couldn't go any further. This couldn't be anything more than a thank-you kiss. Nick had resisted. He'd resisted more than he'd responded because he'd seen the danger.

Lightning flashed around them. The wind blew the trees sideways. It was dark, so dark. Like night had fallen in the middle of the afternoon.

Nick was warm and solid beneath her. His arms strong around her, his grip firm on the steering wheel. Her body reacted to his, whether she liked it or not. There was a connection. A connection she put down to compassion. He'd suffered, but he hadn't gotten off as lightly as she'd thought. It was an accident. An accident he'd caused, but one attributed to the condition of the road. Nick hadn't mentioned that. He hadn't tried to deflect the blame, unlike his lawyer, who had used it to full effect to avoid the careless driving charge for his client.

The man she'd come to know was a different man from the arrogant jerk Charliese had described. He was more likeable than she'd expected. They had a connection of sorts. An unwanted connection that couldn't go anywhere. Not when Carmie adored Nick. This had to stop. This had to stop before her heart had other ideas and it got complicated.

Date five, she told herself. Pretend this is date five. No way would she allow herself to harbour feelings for a man beyond date five. Let go. Disconnect. Water poured down the window of the cab and the tractor engine roared, but Emily pictured herself on a deserted beach in the sunshine, the harsh cry of a seagull above. She was happy on the sand. Warm. Happy. And alone.

Chapter Five

Nick pushed the vehicle to its maximum thrust. They needed to get out of the storm. The wind howled like a rabid wolf and the rain pelted down in vast horizontal sheets that shrouded the land. The road was a quagmire. Water rushed in torrents, gouging the unsealed surface. A lighter vehicle would have been washed away, but the locals knew better than to be out in this. He turned into his driveway and the light from his house shone like a beacon through the dark haze.

He didn't want to think about that kiss. He didn't want to think about Emily invading his home or how he'd never get her presence out again. She'd haunt him forever. Like Charliese. Two beautiful women. Both out of reach. Except Emily wasn't out of reach. She was on his lap, snuggled against him, her warmth penetrating the icy cold. Never had he been so determined to protect a woman. Bring it on, he sneered at the storm. I'm up for it. I won't fail her. Because he had no plans beyond getting her dry, getting her warm and getting her home. His goals were achievable. Manageable. Realistic.

Still, he breathed a sigh of relief when the shed loomed in front of them and he pressed the remote for the huge sliding door. It moved to the side and they blasted in on the fiery breath of the storm. The door struggled to close against the whipping gusts of the wind and the thunderous clap of sound that seemed to suck all the air out of the sheltered space.

Nick turned off the ignition and they were plunged into darkness. The absence of the throbbing engine was barely audible over the relentless barrage of rain against the corrugated iron of the roof and the Colourbond steel walls. The cacophony of sound increased when he opened the door to the cab and Emily extracted herself.

Nick took a deep breath of the fraught air, like he hadn't breathed the entire way home. His thoughts spun and his eyes heated with tears. Thank God, they were back. Emily had fitted against him like she'd been made to fit there. Except she hadn't. She deserved better. She could have died, and he would have had another woman's watery death on his conscience.

Near blinded by the darkness, he wrapped an arm around Emily's shaking body and propelled her towards the side door. He pulled at the door, but the storm pulled back and he had to use both hands—and his body—to create a gap for them to pass through. He took Emily's hand in his and they struggled across the yard to the house, heads bowed, drenched by the sideways rain. It was barely fifty metres, but the distance seemed interminable. By the time they got to the back door and into the warmth of the coat room, they were freshly wet through to the skin.

Nick peeled Emily out of the wet blankets and towels. She struggled out of her saturated coat and grappled with her boots. Water poured out of them and formed puddles on the polished concrete floor. He dragged his own boots off, along with his drenched coat and beanie. So, cold. So, wet.

"You'll be warm soon. Watch out for Alfie. He's still learning his manners." There was a fire in the hearth, and he stirred the wood, the glowing embers sparking into flame. Alfie danced around Emily and took off on a crazy lap around the open plan space, going too fast and knocking into the furniture. "He's mad. Crazy." As crazy as Nick was to have brought Emily here. This was lunacy. He added some more split logs and the flames devoured them greedily. Emily looked like a mermaid, who'd been washed up on the shore, her beautiful face marred with dirt, her hair a scraggly, muddy mess. She looked done in. Exhausted. The rigid resistance in his chest softened. "Let's get you warm."

Her teeth chattered, and she shivered, her lips near purple with the cold. He took her into his arms and held her there until the spasms calmed. "I'll make you a hot chocolate. Here. Sit. Until you warm up." He pointed to the black marble hearth, warmed by the fire. Alfie settled himself at her feet, his head resting on her knee. Her face looked golden with the radiating heat. She patted Alfie's head with long, soothing strokes and another knot in Nick's body untangled and eased.

His fingers burned, the warming blood like blades in his veins. He fumbled with the mugs, knocking the container of chocolate onto its side. *Come on*, he growled. What the hell was wrong with him? The storm raged outside, unleashing its fury against the double-glazed windows which stretched from the floor to the ceiling. He heated milk on the stove, watching vigilantly to avoid it coming to the boil. He wanted it steaming hot and when it was ready, he poured it on top of the chocolate shards and marshmallows, stirring until both mugs were a sweet, swirling, sticky indulgence.

He handed one to Emily, who gratefully cupped it between her hands, her smile lighting her eyes. He sat beside her, the good side of his face to the flames, the warmth of the hearth seeping through the wetness of his jeans.

Emily looked around the open space, her gaze on the cow skin rugs that adorned the warm concrete floor, the leather lounges, the lofty cathedral ceilings. It was a masculine space, decorated to his taste. If she hadn't appreciated his wealth before, she would now. His home was opulent, enormous and self-indulgent, a feature he hadn't appreciated until he saw it through her eyes, but it was his home. His retreat. His castle on the hill. The view was vast and on a good day, he looked across the grass and the hills to the sea and beyond.

"Your home is incredible. Even better on the inside than the outside, which is saying something because I love what you designed and built." Her expression was wistful.

"I wanted privacy. When I lived in LA, it was hard to find."

"Do you think you'll go back to acting?"

"No." His tone was like the blade of a guillotine. Sharp. Snappy. Certain. Never again would he feel comfortable in front of a camera. He wasn't comfortable in front of a mirror let alone enlarged on a movie screen, his scar in cinematic colour, his guilt there for everyone to see.

"What about directing? Producing? Screenwriting."

Her questions brought a flush of heat and a light sheen of sweat to his brow. "I've written some scripts. A couple have been optioned for a television series. I have an idea for a movie, too. Writing suits me. I can do it from here. The internet brings the world to me."

"You've become a recluse." Her tone was soft and reflective. Gentle.

"Maybe, but for now, that's what I want."

"Space and time to heal?" She studied him with dark, caring

eyes. "Or are you hiding from the world?"

"A bit of both." Was he hiding? At first, he'd hidden because he couldn't stand to look in a mirror, let alone see judgement or pity in people's eyes. Now, he still couldn't stand to look in a mirror, or see judgement or pity in people's eyes. Particularly eyes that gazed at him from a perfect face. Emily was a living exclamation mark to all of the reasons he wanted to keep to himself. He was a beast. Inside and out. She could do better than him. And she was too smart to give her heart to the likes of Phillip. Or too afraid. She didn't trust anyone with a Y chromosome, which was some kind of irony. Her five-date rule was a revelation and he shouldn't have felt relieved, but he did, because it meant she wouldn't fall for Phillip.

What did he care if she did?

He sipped his drink and they settled into silence, the storm rampaging outside like a monstrous beast, shaking the walls and clawing at the windows.

"I'll run you a hot bath. You can soak up to your chin and thaw out." He lowered his mug to the hearth and stood. Emily looked ethereal and there was nothing he would have liked more than to cup her chin with his hands and taste her properly, but every cell in his body shied away. *You shouldn't have kissed her. You shouldn't have gone there. She deserves better than you.*

"Nick."

He turned towards her, his body churning with all that he wanted and all that he couldn't have.

"Thank you for saving us. You surprised me, too. You're not the man I thought you were."

She smiled, and his heart swelled in his chest. But when he moved towards the guest bathroom, his thoughts mocked and taunted him. *That doesn't mean she trusts you. That doesn't make you worthy of her. That doesn't mean anything beyond gratitude.*

The water pounded into the bathtub and his head pounded with reasons to back off. He poured a generous portion of scented bath salts into the water and headed into his bedroom to collect some track pants and a top, along with a warm, fleece-lined hoodie and thick socks. He didn't have any women's underwear. She'd be naked in his clothes. His body reacted, hard and eager and the feeling was foreign. It had been a long time.

But Emily was here for his protection, not his pleasure. He wouldn't soon forget the fear in her eyes or the eye-rolling fear of the calf. His own fear had near paralysed him. She'd put her life at risk for a calf, which was crazy insane. Who did that? What kind of woman ventured into a quagmire and near drowned in the process of keeping a calf's head above water? A compassionate one. The same kind of woman who put her modelling career on hold to look after her mother and sister. The same kind of woman who put her sister's happiness before her own.

He turned off the tap and checked the temperature of the water.

The same kind of woman who was none too pleased about the way he treated Carmie. She wanted to protect her sister's heart. She didn't want her to get hurt. She thought his friendship was easy come, easy go. He got it. He didn't plan on hurting either one of them, but then he hadn't planned on hurting Charliese either.

He pulled a soft towel out of the cupboard and left it on the counter in the bathroom.

Emily was curled up on the hearth when he returned, her gaze on the flames, her hands wrapped around her mug with

Alfie asleep nearby. His body reacted again and damn it, *that* was not an option. "The bath's ready when you are." His gaze shifted to the sweeping sheets of rain. The tanks would be full. Even the troughs, not fully functional, would capture enough water for his herd to avoid the dangers of the dam while he got that plumbing job finished. He moved it to the top of his to-do list.

Emily stood, her clothes steaming from the fire. "Maybe I could put my clothes in the dryer while I'm in the bath?"

"I've left some track pants and a hoodie out for you, but I could put your smalls in the dryer if you like. They'll dry quickly." The conversation had his insides in knots. Fisherman-type knots, strong enough to keep boats moored in the churning murk of the sea. Emily's eyes churned with plenty, too. Plenty he refused to see. He was just being neighbourly. It was the least he could do after she'd saved his livestock, and if being neighbourly meant drying her smalls, so be it. If being neighbourly meant loaning her clothes and running a bath, so be it.

But, taking a hold of her lacy underthings—her black lacy underthings—and putting them into the dryer felt intimate. Holy cow. She'd been wearing them not minutes before. Against her most private parts. And she was naked with mere walls between them. Not thinking. Not thinking. Not thinking. Of. That.

He pushed them into the steely appliance, unable to get the feel of them out of his memory, flicked the on-switch and headed for the shower. A hot shower, because he was cold to the bone. Who was he kidding? He blasted himself with icy water until his body convulsed. Fine. Lesson learned. Keep it together, man. He flicked the hot water on and sighed with relief.

Emily blushed every time she thought of handing her smalls through the gap in the doorway. Nick had seen her underwear. He'd put them in the dryer. She held her breath and sank under the water. She'd kissed him and he hadn't responded, until he had, and she wasn't sure which was worse. The hot flush to her cheeks roared like wildfire. What had she done? What had she been thinking? She'd been so grateful, so relieved to be safe, she'd let her guard down. He'd held her. They'd connected, but he hadn't wanted the connection any more than she had. Good. Fine. No problem.

But there was a problem, because she couldn't get the memory of his lips against hers—their kiss—out of her head. She couldn't stop her mind from travelling to how safe she'd felt wrapped in his arms. How for the first time in so long, she'd allowed herself to draw on someone else's strength. Someone she had hated. But Nick had suffered—he suffered still—and punished himself and pushed others away. And Charliese had cheated on him. It was a new kind of thought and she turned it over in her mind. He didn't need rescuing. He didn't need or want her pity. He didn't need or want her at all.

Charliese's affair had been more of a fling—an escape—and it wasn't rare in the world they inhabited. Humans were vain, insecure, self-centred creatures and being beautiful was no insurance policy against it. She'd learned that at an early age.

Nick felt responsible for the accident. He *was* responsible. He'd driven recklessly, and he'd paid a terrible price. Charliese had paid a terrible price.

Her heart squeezed in her chest. Was that why she'd kissed him? Had she kissed him out of pity? No. He'd suffered, but he wasn't weak. He was damaged, but he wasn't broken. He was isolated, but he wasn't a pariah. And he'd shown kindness to Carmie. He cared, not only for his neighbours, but his animals and his farm. So maybe she'd kissed him out of relief and gratitude. She'd held the calf's head out of the water, but she couldn't have rescued it. Hell, she'd needed rescuing herself. If Nick hadn't come? She sank under the water and stayed there in the silence of no breath until her lungs screamed, her thoughts spun, and panic clawed at her insides. She broke the still surface, gasping for air, water splashing over the sides of the bath. If Nick hadn't come, she would have drowned. They both would have drowned. He saved her life.

Her mind turned to the morning she'd arrived and the man she'd met on the ferry. The reek of alcohol and the state of his face. That man wasn't the man she'd come to know.

She sank back under the water in frustration, and her mind flashed to Charliese. She should get out. She was past warm to the point of hot, but what if it wasn't safe to go home? She couldn't stay overnight. Not now. That kiss had changed things. There was an attraction between them. An attraction neither one of them wanted.

There was a knock on the door. "Em, I've left your things out here for you when you're ready."

Emily jumped, startled to hear Nick's voice so close. "Thanks," she called back, her mouth sand-dry, her heart pounding, her body naked.

Nick busied himself in the kitchen. Hot soup was what they needed. He chopped the vegetables and threw the onion and garlic into the pot, the olive oil sizzling and spitting. Then the celery and the carrot. Sweet potato. Vegetable stock. Pumpkin and a can of lentils rinsed clean. He stirred the concoction and sprinkled in salt and pepper, some hot paprika, and chopped chives and parsley. By the time he heard Emily at the doorway, he'd cleared away the debris and poured himself a wine.

"Would you like a glass?" He saw a flash of concern in her chocolate gaze before she turned to the bank of windows where the rain pelted against them like an encore.

"No, thanks. Just water would be great. The weather is crazy out there." She settled herself on a stool at the island bench, her hair wet, her cheeks pink.

His heart flipped in his chest.

"Something smells good." She eyed the pot on the stove. "You really do know your way around a kitchen, Wheatley."

She looked good in his clothes. It felt good… with her in his kitchen. "I thought I should feed you." He busied himself with her water, grateful for something to do with his hands. "Lentil and vegetable soup."

"Sounds lovely, thank you."

He'd put on his favourite music and the haunting sound of Enya filled the silence. It felt like a date, which was ridiculous. If he could go back and change that moment when her lips had clung to his and he'd kissed her despite a chorus of misgivings, he would. Or maybe it was handling her underwear. Or seeing her in his clothes. Something had changed between them. There was a level of intimacy, and it felt anything but neighbourly.

"Do you think the weather will improve enough for me to go home?"

"Not according to the radar." He pushed her glass of water across the marble island bench top. "But don't worry, I have a guest room and a spare pair of pyjamas. A new toothbrush."

And a damn lock on the door he hoped she'd use. Not that she'd need it for he fully planned to lock his own door and shackle himself to the bed.

"I'd better let Mum know."

"I called her while you were in the bath. Phillip answered the phone and he was none too pleased about it, but it's not safe to go out in this. Carmie said to look after you, which I fully plan to do."

"What about their dinner? They need vegies to go with the roast."

"I'm sure they'll manage." Typical of Emily to think of her family before herself.

"I'm sorry about earlier…" She sipped her drink and her cheeks flushed pink. "I was so relieved to be safe that… I forgot myself for a moment. I'm not interested in…" Her fingers twisted around the glass, but her chocolate gaze held his, brave and defiant. "I'm not interested in a relationship with you or anyone else."

"I'm not interested in a relationship either." He should have felt relieved. He should have been grateful to her for bringing the awkward out into the open, but his stomach dipped, and he realised he was disappointed. *Get over it, mate. It was never a thing. It was a thank-god-I'm-safe kiss. At best, a thank-you kiss. At worst, a pity kiss.*

"Are you okay?" Her deep ochre gaze searched his.

He wanted to fight. He wanted to shake her into admitting what he knew deep down to be true. She was attracted to him.

No. She pities you.

She's attracted to me. Somehow, this beautiful woman was attracted to him, scars and all. At least enough to kiss him.

It was a pity kiss. She deserves better than you.

"What about a game of Monopoly? Cards? Chess?"

"Sure. I love Monopoly. I've played it with Carmie for years, so you'll have to be good if you want to beat me."

"Now there's a challenge if I've ever heard one." And so was the five-date rule. It was like insider trading. None of the men she dated knew their dates were numbered. He had an advantage if he wanted to make this a thing instead of a mistake, which he didn't.

Or maybe he did.

He sought out the Monopoly box and set it up on the timber dining table, portioning bank notes to either side of the board. "Which token would you like?"

"The racing car." Her response was quick like it was her favourite piece and she fossicked for it amongst the small stack of tokens.

"Hmmm. What does that say about you, I wonder?"

"That I like fast cars? What piece do you want?" She placed hers on *Go*.

He used to like fast cars, too. His gut twisted and knotted. "I'll be the money bag. Let *that* be a warning!"

"Oh, I'm going to enjoy every minute of beating you." She settled his piece beside hers.

"Fighting words." He took a sip of his wine and her forehead creased. She looked past him to the window, indecision in her eyes.

Lightning flashed, splintering the sky.

"What is it?" His insides tightened and he lowered his glass to the table.

"Do you often... Are you...?" Her gaze dropped to the board, then lifted back to his. "Are you an alcoholic?"

"No." His tone was shocked. Defensive. "Why would you

think that?" He threw the dice and landed a five and a six. He picked them up and passed them over to her. The touch of her hand was warm, but her eyes were cool.

"The morning I arrived, you stank like a brewery and looked like you'd spent the night getting cosy with a bottle or ten. I wasn't sure whether to get in the car with you, to be honest. Charliese told me you drank… a lot. And today, you pulled out a whiskey flask. Tonight, wine."

Emily threw two sixes. What were the chances?

"The flask was my dad's and he always kept it on the tractor, for medicinal purposes only. Tonight? I was being polite. I haven't had a guest here for so long it seemed fitting." He took a deep breath, fought to settle the erratic kerthump in his chest, and shuffled the Chance and Community Chest cards. "I rarely drink alone. I'd say never, but last weekend was a first." He stacked the cards and put them in the middle of the board. "I finally found the courage to visit Charliese's grave. Two years after the accident. And you're right. I did find a bottle or ten to keep me company that night. It was a very rough day." Alfie rested his head on Nick's knee, and he stroked his smooth, silky coat.

"I'm sorry. I was wrong to judge you. That must have been difficult." Her gaze held his, haunted with shadows. A log shifted and collapsed in the fireplace and sparks hissed. "I used to arrive home from school to a very drunk mum more times than I care to remember. I cleaned up her vomit. I bathed her. I washed her clothes. I looked after Carmie. An alcoholic bender is a red flag, a neon sign, a burning cross."

"I might have drunk myself stupid that night, but I hadn't touched a drop of alcohol since the accident. I used to drink too much and Charliese was right. I was a fool." He didn't blame Emily for the misgivings etched into her brow and many things made more sense. Like how she was so adept at running a household. Like how she was more of a mum to Carmie than a sister. Like how she'd been closed and cold in her attitude towards him. He'd assumed it was because of Charliese, but it ran deeper than that. There was her dad, who'd left her to struggle alone… and her mum had been an alcoholic? His mind turned to that first morning and he saw himself from her perspective. No wonder she'd mistrusted him. No wonder she'd worried about him spending time with Carmie.

"I'm glad to hear it."

"I'm glad to say it."

"It must have been hard, seeing the gravestone."

Her gaze studied his, liquid with what? Pity? Sadness? Understanding. The thought crept over him like a cold breeze. His skin prickled and puckered in a wave that travelled from his head to his feet. She knew. She knew what was written on it. Of course, she knew.

"Yes, it was." His gaze lowered to her right hand and the bare finger where the ring so like his wife's had been. He hadn't imagined it. He had to ask, but Emily threw the dice and the moment was gone.

She landed a pair of threes and moved the car, settling on The Angel, Islington. "Buy it." Her eyes brightened and she flashed him a triumphant smile before waving some bank notes towards him. "Do you want to be banker, or shall we help ourselves?"

"Help yourself. I trust you." His thoughts clashed. His mind rattled. He did trust her. She had integrity and boundaries and had somehow navigated the modelling world without falling for the dangers. Alcohol for one. Men like Phillip for two.

She'd answered some of the questions that lurked when he allowed them to. And she hadn't left that kiss hanging between them. She'd cleared up the confusion. She'd let him off the hook. He should be grateful. His skin settled. The jerky beat of his heart settled. The clanging in his ears quieted. He stroked Alfie's head and the warmth of the room, the sound of the music, the magic of the wine worked its charm.

"I appreciate that." Her gaze steadied on his and the air between them sparked with an electrical storm of their own. She took the card for the property and smiled at him. Not a victorious smile or a gloating one. More of a soft, whimsical smile. "Did you know this property isn't named after a street? The Angel was a pub, a coaching inn. It's even mentioned by Charles Dickens in Oliver Twist." She lowered her gaze and her cheeks flushed. "In my world, there's only one kind of angel—a Victoria's Secret Angel. And she's a force. More like a warrior than a woman. I've always wanted to be one." She settled the card on the table and rethrew the dice. Another double. "Twelve." She zoomed around the board and landed on Marlborough Street. "Buy it."

"You'll fit right in and trust me, you're already a force." He picked up his wine, sat back and sipped. Her smile was more demon than angel and the power of it churned his insides. "Let me know when you're done. I get the feeling you don't need me."

She stopped mid-cashier motion and her eyes confirmed everything he'd guessed. She didn't need a man. She didn't need the complications that buzzed between them like a million mosquitos. And he didn't need them either.

Another throw. This time a three. "Buy it." Emily smiled and slipped the Strand into her property line-up.

"I hope you've got enough money left for Mayfair." He always kept a handy four hundred dollars in reserve just in case. Mayfair was the cream of the properties and he liked the cream.

Emily looked like the cat who'd eaten the cream as she handed over the dice and took a sip of her water. "I've got plenty left and who knows, you might have to pay rent."

Smug. Confident. A woman who knew her power. He'd do well to remember it. Was this about vengeance for her friend? Was that what the damn kiss was about? To soften him up? To weaken his resistance? Then reject him?

She doesn't want you. She's not interested in damaged goods. She could have any man on the planet. She's got plans. Goals. Big ones.

Perhaps he should be the banker.

Perhaps he couldn't trust her.

But what buzzed between them was palpable, the air as taut as the wire he'd used to repair his damaged fence. His senses heightened. His body reacted. The feelings might be foreign, but he knew attraction when he felt it. He had no interest in a one-night fling. He didn't want the five-date special either. And he sure as heck didn't want her pity.

He wanted more.

No, he didn't. Damn it, she messed with his mind. He didn't want a woman in his life.

He might want *this* woman in his life.

He threw the dice with a little more force than was necessary and one ended up on the floor, which reminded him of Carmie. Three. He eyed the board. Whitechapel Road. "Buy it." He feigned excitement for they both knew it was one of the cheapest properties on the board, but a man had to start somewhere, and he'd take what he could get.

Besides, he had a beautiful woman sitting opposite him, snug in his clothes, and the promise of a delicious evening ahead with company instead of silence. Emily filled his home with warmth and now *he* felt like the cat who'd eaten the cream. He rummaged for his property card with a smile on his face. "Your turn."

Emily watched the emotions wash over Nick's face. If she read him right, he hadn't known about the baby and the knowing had sent him to a bar to nurse his sorrows. She, too, had cried when she'd seen the epitaph, but she was glad Charliese's parents had chosen to acknowledge the small life who had died in her womb.

But why had it taken him two years to visit Charliese's grave?

He hadn't been able to attend the funeral because he was still in hospital and there had been relief all around. She'd been free to mourn the loss of her closest friend without having to tiptoe around the man who had killed her. But if Charliese hadn't told him about the baby, then he wouldn't have known. He hadn't known and the results of his self-flagellation had been hard to witness.

Emily threw the dice with renewed vigour and bought another property. She eyed her stack of cash. She had enough money if she landed on Mayfair. She glanced at Nick. His gaze was steady on hers and her heart jolted in her chest.

"Can I ask about the ring?" His blue gaze swam with questions. "The ring you had on the other day." His gaze dropped to her bare finger. "Was that Charliese's engagement ring?"

So, he had noticed. She'd been right to take it off. It had seemed insensitive to wear it after he'd been so kind. "Yes. She gave it to me and insisted I wear it to remind me to protect my heart…"

That love and lust are synonymous with loss and loathing.

"… I don't need the reminder. I learned at a young age that there was no such thing as a Prince Charming who would come to my rescue. But I promised I'd wear it." She wore it still… on a chain around her neck, tucked carefully under her clothing.

Charliese hadn't loved him. Not at the end. She'd married Nick in a haze of lust, and Emily could see the danger. *But if Charliese had lived? She would have left him. She'd planned to divorce him. She hadn't loved him any more than he'd loved her.*

Emily's thoughts veered from one argument to the next. But Charliese hadn't lived and Emily's attraction to Nick seemed like a betrayal.

"I thought it might have been hers." His tone was raw, his eyes haunted, and memories swarmed between them.

Emily pulled the chain from beneath her clothing and over her head. "It's rightfully yours."

Nick wasn't the man she'd thought he was. He wasn't the man Charliese had described. He'd helped her mum and befriended her sister. And that unsettled her more than the rest.

"If Charliese wanted you to have it, then *I* want you to have it. I'm grateful she had a friend like you to turn to." He pushed the ring back towards her. "But I want you to know that when I gave Charliese this ring, I loved her…or at least I thought I loved her. It was only after the accident I could see the truth. I wasn't capable of love and neither was she."

"I'm sorry it didn't work out."

"Me, too."

Nick picked up the dice and threw them, landing on a Chance

square. He slipped a card from the top of the stack and waved it in her direction. *"Take a walk on the boardwalk, advance token to Mayfair."*

"No way!"

"You don't believe me?"

"Show me the card, Wheatley." Her words were a throaty growl.

"Interesting." Nick's tone was contemplative as he placed the card face up on the board and moved his token to Mayfair. So, she didn't trust him. She didn't trust him with a Chance card, let alone her heart. "Buy it," he gloated, waving a five-hundred-dollar bill towards her. "Although I might consider selling. How much are you willing to offer?" His mind went to places it really shouldn't have. Strip Monopoly? A shared bed? There were plenty of suggestions that came to mind. None of them decent. None of them neighbourly. Just how far would she go to get something she set her sights on? It was an interesting question.

Emily pondered her cash, then her gaze—like decadent chocolate—returned to his.

"It turns out I don't want Mayfair as much as I thought I did."

His pulse thudded. Was she talking about Mayfair or was she talking about that kiss? She didn't want him? His heart banged against his ribs. Or was he misreading her? That kiss had scrambled his brain and his lower body reacted. Again. Still.

"I can beat you without it. Besides, you don't have Park Lane." She slipped the necklace back over her head and tucked it under her top. Black shadows darkened her eyes and her lips pressed together.

"Neither do you."

He'd put that ring on Charliese's finger within weeks of meeting her—a mistake as it turned out—and she'd stepped away from her career, her friends, her family. He'd wanted her all to himself. Their beach wedding had seemed romantic. Just the two of them and a celebrant. He hadn't wanted the public fiasco. The media. The drama. He'd wanted privacy. In truth, he hadn't wanted to share her. He'd wanted to own her. The knowledge turned his stomach. Emily should have hated him on sight.

Emily *had* hated him on sight.

He'd killed not only his wife, but his child. Shame burned in every cell of his body and his gaze clung to the board. He moved his piece, but his stomach churned. He dealt with the bank and the real estate cards, but his insides shrivelled and curled, and he struggled to lift his gaze back to hers. To face what he'd done. To face the woman who knew—who knew—what a poor excuse of a man he was.

And yet she'd kissed him. Attraction sparked between them. From his side alone?

"My turn." Emily reached for the dice.

Her face was serene, a beautiful mask, but he knew better. Perhaps he'd underestimated her. Perhaps she wanted him to suffer. Perhaps that kiss had been about playing him for a fool. And he'd fallen for it. All of it. She didn't want him. She wasn't attracted to him. She wanted retribution. And he didn't blame her.

He reached for his wine and took a gulp.

Emily threw the dice and moved her token around the board. Her hands were beautiful—slender—her skin, golden and satiny smooth.

She landed on Park Lane with a smug smile and a "Whoo hoo."

She counted out her cash and sifted through the diminishing stack for the property card. "Bring it on, Wheatley."

Bring it on indeed.

Chapter Six

"You must be tired." Nick could see Emily's exhaustion. She was done in, but there was a companionable truce of sorts between them and he was loath to disturb it. With the storm raging outside and the fire glowing inside, the room was a softly lit cocoon, cosy and warm. Alfie lay asleep at his feet and they each nursed a hot chocolate in front of the dancing flames.

"My body aches in places I didn't know I had." Her voice was a soft burr, like she was comfortable and relaxed.

"They're big beasts, even the baby ones."

"Thank you for your kind hospitality." Her gaze was warm, friendly even.

"You're welcome." They'd had a good night, and her joy at winning Monopoly had outweighed his chagrin at losing. He found he liked her in his space. A lot. Too much. He was past a fool. He could see her here. He could imagine their life together as a couple. A married couple. And that's when his head got involved with scathing words that left his heart smarting.

"Nick, I…" Emily stopped speaking and studied the flames. The light flashed and waned as the centre of a log disintegrated into a shower of sparks. The sound drew his attention away from her and he stood to stoke the dry wood at the periphery into the centre of the action. He loaded a marshmallow onto a long-handled fork and passed it to her.

"Thank you." She settled herself on the hearth and held the marshmallow close to the bright red embers until it caught flame. She blew it out and tasted, her eyes closing to savour the sweetness.

The force of his reaction left him weak, scarcely able to lift his more carefully charred marshmallow to his mouth. Soft and gooey and good. He didn't remember the last time he'd toasted marshmallows and he realised he'd let these moments slide. The small moments. The small moments that in hindsight were so big.

His mum had seen what he hadn't. His need to reconnect with nature. His need for time to heal, to appreciate the lessons he'd learned, and now he realised that every pain-filled moment had brought him here, to this moment, with this woman.

"Nick, I…" Her eyes were shiny with tears. "I loved Charliese, I did, but she should have told you about the baby. I'm sorry you had to find out the way you did."

His body went rigid, like someone had poured quick-set concrete from above and he found himself entrapped in a concrete tomb. He couldn't breathe. He couldn't move. He couldn't expand his lungs far enough to grapple for air. His head spun. His vision darkened.

"I knew about the affair. I knew she planned to leave you." Emily stabbed another marshmallow onto her fork. "I knew about the baby."

Every word felt like a dagger. A blade that cut through the concrete like it was butter. Every word found its home.

"You were a lousy husband. Unfaithful. Self-centred."

Her marshmallow caught fire and she blew it out, her gaze mesmerised by the flames.

He dragged a breath into his paralysed lungs. "I don't expect you to forgive me. Actually, I don't know how you can bear to be in the same room with me." His voice croaked like it had shattered along with his heart and his soul in the mirror she'd held up for him. He didn't need it. He knew the monster she described. And yet here she was. Alone with him in his monster's lair. "Why did you kiss me? If you knew all of this. Why did you kiss me?"

She turned to him, her lashes wet, her eyes shadowed in the soft light.

His body shook and his throat burned. He dropped his head into his hands and gave in to the gut-wrenching pain. His child. He'd killed his own child. He'd been unfaithful to his wife. His driving had killed her, whether he'd been at fault or not. He was beyond deserving of forgiveness. Emily knew what he was. She saw him. She knew. Yet here she sat, beside him.

Alfie licked at his hands and his tears. Tears. He was a great, wussy, crying, pathetic monster of a man who didn't deserve to survive the accident.

"Nick."

Her voice was close to his ear and it took some time for him to realise she'd wrapped her arm around him and sat close beside him, her leg tucked in against his. Why hadn't she left? Emily was brave enough and strong enough to face any storm. But she'd stayed. The thought was slow to crystallise and when it did, he lifted his head and grappled for the tissues she held out to him. He hadn't cried. He hadn't cried since he'd read the gravestone, and the tears had been building up inside him like a storm threatening to break and the breaking had been a relief, but breaking in front of Emily? He felt more monster than man. More mouse, than lion. "It's time I went to bed." Alone. Loneliness stretched before him like an endless highway through a fathomless desert.

"I'm sorry for your loss. I'm sorry this happened to you. Your face. Charliese. It's time to put it behind you. You've suffered enough."

His child. He'd killed his child. He could never suffer enough.

"Thank you. I'm sorry. I haven't cried in a long time. I guess... I guess I needed to. Your kindness is more than I deserve." He stood up and dug his hands into his pockets. He wanted to be alone. "Let me show you to your room."

He put the fire-screen in front of the fire and settled Alfie into his basket. Emily reached for his hand and he held it like a lifeline. Her hand was warm. Her skin, smooth. Her grip, tight. Like she wouldn't let him go. The night lights along the passage gave them enough light to see, but not enough to illuminate the ugliness he was. He led her towards the room he'd prepared for her. The storm was waning beyond the windows, the rain steady, the wind more of a moan than a howl, a heavy breath against the glass. When he got to the door of the guest room, he flicked on the light and turned to her. "Good-night, Em. The ensuite is stocked and you should find everything you need."

"Not everything I need. Not if you're planning to leave." Her words were soft and whispered.

His skin prickled and his throat tightened until he thought he'd choke.

"I can't bear for you to be alone. Not tonight. Not when I'm here and there's no need for it." She stood stubbornly close.

"I don't need your pity." His tone was like cut glass. Jagged. Dangerous. "I don't want your pity." His words came to his ears from a distance, like they'd travelled down the passage to his room and locked the door behind them.

"I'm not offering you pity. I'm offering you company. Comfort."

"Why did you kiss me?"

"You saved my life."

"That hardly makes up for the lives I didn't save."

"It was an accident, Nick. The court ruled it an unfortunate accident. I have the newspaper cut-outs to prove it."

"It was my fault. I was driving. I couldn't get her free." The words travelled on a sob, a great wave of a sob, and Emily drew him into her arms and held him close. Her warmth seeped into him, and her heart beat strong and solid against him. He breathed her in, her scent, sweet and musky. The snarl of his thoughts, the knot in his gut, released and loosened.

"Stay with me. Let me hold you. Just hold you." Her tone was gentle.

He stepped back. His eyes welled and he cursed his weakness. "I'd like that, but I don't deserve it. I deserve to sleep alone."

"You've suffered enough." She rested her hand against his cheek. His damaged cheek.

Nick cringed for he knew what she felt, what she must see, yet her gaze was on his and it was warm and loving and caring. He didn't deserve her. He didn't deserve the peace that settled inside him like the storm had blown itself out. Like his inside world was bathed in sunlight. Weak through the clouds. But warm and nourishing and healing.

"I'll go and get organised for bed." His voice was thin like something clutched at his throat.

"Don't leave."

Her smile was beautiful. Ethereal. And he couldn't resist its light. His heart banged in his chest and his ears roared with the rush of his blood, the surge of his pulse. "Are you sure?"

"Yes." She let go of his hand, but her gaze clung to his. He couldn't leave. It was like a magnetic field. She was one hell of a force. A force he couldn't deny.

He stepped closer and drew her against him. His lips found hers and her arms wrapped around him until she nestled against him, soft to his hard. He couldn't find the words, but his kiss spoke of everything he felt. It wasn't a frivolous, light-hearted kind of kiss, but the kind that stirred his soul. A connection. A conduit. A joining of more than lips and mouths. A tasting that was slow and gentle and seeking. A hunger that caught and lit and burned. Every stroke of her tongue had him hankering for more. He tasted like a man starved. Like she was the only woman he'd ever wanted. Like she was the only woman who'd ever touched him this far inside. Never had a kiss left him so feather light. So joyously lost. So wondrously found. And when she drew away, his mouth followed hers and he tasted again like he couldn't bear to disconnect for even a heartbeat. She smiled, her lips soft and smooth against his and he couldn't help but smile, too. Her eyes reflected all that he felt, and he kissed her again, short and sharp like a punctuation mark. He cupped his hands around her face and studied the darkness of her eyes. "Are you sure about this? You don't have to…"

"Do you want me to change my mind, Wheatley?"

"No." His answer was gun-fire quick. She took his hand and drew him into the room. The lamplight was soft, and her scent curled around him like a spell or a curse. Sweet. Sweet. Sweet and spicy. Sweet and dangerous. She offered comfort, nothing more, and he was grateful. They didn't need the complication of a physical relationship… but there was nothing neighbourly about the way she looked at him and nothing neighbourly about the way he wanted her.

He pulled back the bed covers, and they curled up together, his gaze on hers. He breathed in the delicious scent of her hair and buried his nose in its silken softness. How the hell was he going to sleep when his body was going off like a firecracker, hard and crazy and begging for something he barred from his mind. It was enough that she was there. It was enough to have her warm beside him. And he hoped, for once, he would get through the night without drowning.

"Nick?"

"Yep?"

There was a pause as if she wanted to say something but thought better of it. "I'm glad I'm here. I'm glad you're not alone."

He pulled the bed covers over them and turned off the light. They'd had a big day and Emily found sleep before he did. He listened to the soft flow of her breath and savoured every moment of her closeness. Nick counted sheep. Literally. He pictured their woolly bodies and got to about a thousand before he slipped off to sleep with Emily snuggled against him.

Emily woke to Nick thrashing in the bed beside her, his voice a yell.

"I've got you. No! You're stuck." His voice cracked. "I can't get you free." Sobs came. Deep, heart-wrenching sobs.

Emily stroked his hair and kissed his sweating forehead. "Nick. Wake up. It's a dream. Wake up." She shook him, but he fought her. "I can't get you. I can't get you out."

"It's alright, Nick. You tried. I know you did your best."

"It wasn't enough." His voice broke and the tears came, waves of them.

"It's done. There's nothing you can do. It's over." She drew him close and held his head against her chest, whispering soothing words into his warm, damp hair. His pain was there, in his rigid body, in the knotted muscles, in his wracking sobs.

"It'll never be over."

"How often?" she asked. "How often do you have this nightmare?"

"Every night, but sometimes it's me who's drowning, and I can't get out. I'm trapped in the car and I hear my own voice… But I can't breathe, and the water fills my lungs and then I wake up gasping and desperate for air."

She wiped the wetness from his cheeks and sought his mouth. "I can't bear your pain."

"No one can. It's mine to bear. Alone."

"You're not alone. Not tonight." He was a good man. Deep down. He was a good man. Bad things happened to good people. Maybe love truly was blind and crazy-stupid. Her mum had loved her father, which kind of proved it. And right now, every cell in her body wanted to make him feel better. She pressed her mouth to his and he kissed her like he was starved and only she could sustain him. Like he was thirsting and only she could quench him. Like he was adrift and only she could save him. She kissed him with everything she had. She poured herself into him and met him—mind, body, and soul—in a place where there was just the two of them. Where the world was sunny and warm, and the sea was quiet and turquoise, and they could see to the sandy bottom, the fish colourful and serene.

She saw his pain. She felt it and tasted it and heard it. She sensed it with every cell in her body. Every stroke of their tongues, every greedy touch of his hands against her, every greedy touch of her hands against him made their connection more thorough, more infinite, more endless. She wanted him like she'd never wanted a man before. With her soul. And she rushed to explore every curve, every hard plane of his body, with her hands, with her mouth, with her teeth. She tore at his clothes until his chest was bare, sending blasts of reaction to every corner of her body. He tore at hers until they were naked. Until she could feel him, skin against skin. He groaned. He sighed. He breathed her name. His touch brought an answering cry of her own. He was close, but not nearly close enough. She pressed herself against him, the hair on his legs rough against hers, the hair on his chest, pure provocation. She rolled onto him and pressed her mouth against his.

"You're very tasty, Wheatley," she said with a purr.

"You're pretty tasty yourself, Stone."

"I want to see you."

"No."

His movement stopped, and he went rigid beneath her. "I'm sorry. I forgot."

"How could you forget?"

"Easily. You're more than a face to me, and I hope I'm more than a face to you."

"Hell, yes."

"Then fine. I don't need to see you. I'm kind of enjoying the feel of you anyway. And you're right. Why would I want to see you when I can taste you?" She ran her tongue over the top of his lip.

"I'll put the light on, because your face is to die for, but it doesn't come close to being the thing I like most about you."

"What's the thing you like most about me?"

"I kind of like you being on top of me. You're the perfect weight."

"I kind of like you under me."

"Oh, yeah?" He spun her over until he was on top. "What about this? Do you like this?"

His lower body pressed into her belly and she couldn't say she didn't like it. "Hmmm. Not bad."

"Not bad?"

"It could be better."

"You think?"

He pressed his mouth to hers and she tasted him like tomorrow didn't exist. Like nothing existed except this moment. And he kissed her back like a man in a hurry. She writhed beneath him and he drove her to the brink of insanity, until her craving for him became a tormented scream in her head.

"Wait. I'll be back."

He rolled away and flicked the lamp switch, bathing soft light over the bed, and with a grin, he disappeared out of the door. She was shell-shocked for the longest moment until he skidded back through the doorway and leapt onto her, his mouth taking hers in a hungry kiss, before travelling to her breast and tasting with provocative heat, his hands worshipping her like he'd been gone for a hundred days rather than a hundred seconds. Sensation arced through her body and the fire that had raged between her thighs leapt back into insatiable life. She dragged him against her and whispered into his mouth. "Please, Wheatley. Can we get on with this?"

"Are you sure? Because I don't want you to regret this in the morning."

Her hands tangled in his hair and she pulled him back to where she wanted him. Mouth to mouth. Skin to skin. Eye to eye.

"I won't regret it. I'd promise you the life of my first child if it would make you move, preferably inside me. Preferably sooner rather than later…before I incinerate, and you're left with nothing but ashes."

His movement stilled.

"I'm sorry. So stupid of me. How could I say that? My brain is fried. You do that to me. You leave me in a spin. Come on, Nick, please." She cupped her hands around his face and examined the awful scar. On reflection, it wasn't so awful. But the pain behind it was. The story behind the scar. The man behind the face. "I love your scar because it brought us together. It made you the person you are now. A person I admire. A person I desire. A person I like." She kissed the damaged flesh and closed her eyes as if by willing it, she could heal him. She felt his tears, hot against her mouth, and her heart tore in her chest. Ragged, she gazed into the fierce blue of his eyes, and for the longest moment she drank him in as if he could fill the aching emptiness where loneliness ruled, barren and brutal.

She reached for that part of him that was hard and hungry against her, running her hand over the silken tip and down the thick length. He reacted like he'd been touched by an electric cow prod and she laughed, a soft release that broke the spell that had captured them both. She lowered her mouth to taste his neck, his chest, arrowing closer to that part of him that intrigued her. She used her mouth and hands and exalted in her power to make him whimper and cry out. The good kind of crying. She wanted to blot out the bad. She wanted him to feel so good he would never feel bad again. She wanted his body to sing. And when he dragged her off to fumble with protection, her body wept with anticipation. Her soul wept with its need to connect with him… fully, completely, absolutely. She rolled onto him and helped him slide the condom home. "I want you. I really want you. I want you more than I've wanted anyone."

"And I really want you. More than I've wanted anyone. Ever."

Emily slid back until he fitted against her, until all it would take was a rocking motion to meet him in the most intimate way possible. And with her eyes on his in the soft lamplight, they moved together until she couldn't keep her eyes open against the sheer ecstasy of it and she became lost in the movement of his body inside hers, the tantalising friction driving them both higher and higher until her body exploded and pulsed against his and she couldn't have stopped moving if she'd tried. And when her body collapsed against him, his body stiffened, and the throbbing pulse of his release stirred her all over again.

Never had she felt so close to another human soul.

Never had she felt so connected.

Never would she forget the joy she'd found in his arms.

They lay naked together, his arm wrapped possessively around her, and it was like she floated or levitated, so light was her heart. When Nick rolled away to deal with the condom, she missed him like he'd stolen a part of her. When he settled beside her again, he scooped her close and spooned around her. She'd never felt so safe, so cherished, so wanted. And with Nick's breath steady on her neck, she smiled. No more bad dreams. Not tonight anyway, but sex trumped her five-date rule and there was no going back.

Chapter Seven

"Wake up, sleeping beauty. I've made poached eggs on toast, with avocado and my mum's famous chutney." He opened the blind allowing sunlight to spill across the bed.

Emily opened an eye and groaned, the light like a blade. "Every muscle is sore."

"I'll run you a bath. Epsom salts."

"You're all heart." He was chipper and smiling and she wasn't sure which version of him was worse.

"I am." He grinned. "Come on, the sun's out and the rain's gone. Along with half the driveway, but I can deal with that later. Alfie can't wait to see you."

Emily opened the other eye in time for a generous licking. Alfie had followed Nick into the bedroom. "Aghh." She rolled away and swiped the wetness from her cheek. "He's not my favourite kisser."

"He has a definite tongue advantage."

"He's got doggy breath," she muttered, screwing up her face. "What's he been eating?"

"Something dead more than likely. He's a scavenger. Half-seagull. Or at least a distant relative."

"Okay, okay. I give up. Get him away from me. Very

123

underhanded by the way. I could have stayed here all day. It's a very comfy bed." He had that sexy-man-shadow look happening, his hair ruffled and gorgeous. He was dressed in jeans and a black t-shirt and his hair was wet at the ends from the shower. He smelt clean and fresh.

"I need to get you home."

That soaring part of her, faltered. "Are you in a rush to get rid of me?"

"Hardly." He pressed his lips to hers in a very convincing kiss. "Carmie has been on the blower asking when you'll be back. I told her you were still asleep, and she advised me to wake you up, feed you and drive you home. I said, your wish is my command."

"Nice. So just how far would you go to please her?" She snuggled deeper into the warmth of the bed, so cosy, so comfy.

"Not as far as I'd go to please you." He settled himself on the side of the bed and smoothed her hair back from her face, his blue eyes clear and bright. When he smiled, there was a dimple in his cheek on the good side of his face. It was there on the other side, too, not as quick to pucker, but there all the same.

"Hmmph. So, what *are* your intentions with my older sister?"

"I'm thinking best friends. I need to butter her up to tell her I love her sister." His tone was frivolous and jokey, but beneath it was a soft burr. A burr that caught in the hairs on her skin, lifting them and lowering them with fears she didn't want to consider.

"You do? You don't think it's a bit soon for those kinds of feelings? We haven't even been on a date." She answered in kind, her tone jocular, but there was nothing funny about the intensity of his gaze. It burrowed under her skin until she had nowhere to hide.

"We're not dating. Ever."

"Why not?"

"Because your dates are numbered, and I don't plan on stopping at date five. I thought we'd bypass dating and stick with being friends—close friends—for now. Friends who see each other—I'm hoping a lot—but in truth, I don't need to date you to know how I feel."

Emily's playful mood dissipated. He was a man who fell in love quickly—and out of it just as quickly. Charliese's ring on the bedside table glinted in the light. She didn't want that kind of love. She didn't trust that kind of love, even if her body was in full disagreement. She didn't want a relationship full stop. Sex trumped the five-date rule. It was her cue to step away... slowly. Put the nice man down.

He wants a friendship, not a relationship.

Her thoughts tangled. She'd connected with him in a way she hadn't connected with a man before and her body still buzzed and ached from their lovemaking. It was sex and sex she could deal with. It was a physical act. No heart-ship involved.

"Don't overthink it, Stone." He lowered his lips to where her thoughts puckered the skin of her brow. "Come on. Rise and shine. It's breakfast time."

"Soon. I'll come soon." She snuggled deeper into the warmth of the bedding, drawing it up over her nose.

"I didn't take you for a slow-to-wake kind of girl."

"I had disrupted sleep and my dreams were very disturbing."

"Disturbing in a good way or a bad way?"

"Mostly good... and I am kind of hungry." Visions of poached egg and avocado on toast danced before her eyes. "Actually, I'm really hungry. I'm starving. I'm on my way." She pushed the bedding back and reached for his over-sized top, feeling kind of coy in the light of day.

"*Mostly* good, hah? We'll have to fix that. Maybe we should fix that right away."

"No, you don't, Wheatley. I'm a woman in need of sustenance and not the kind you have in mind. I need food. And a shower." He feigned disappointment and she laughed. "You're insatiable."

"I blame you entirely." Nick walked towards the door and Emily took the opportunity to appreciate the tightness of his butt in his jeans. Not that the feel of his butt wasn't etched into her sensory memory, where it would likely never wash away.

He spun at the door and whistled for Alfie who streaked after him, his smile suggesting he'd caught her quiet appreciation.

"No dallying, Stone. Your brekky will get cold."

"I love a man who cooks," she called after him.

"Oh, I love a woman who loves a man who cooks."

Emily laughed and dragged her aching bones from the bed. She visited the bathroom, showered, then slipped into her underwear, and his track pants and warm fleecy. She gazed at the freshly washed world beyond the window. The sky was blue, and the sun shone. The grass glittered like a field of diamonds all the way to the sea. It was like being on top of the world, and her heart sang. She knew the heady aftermath of a good lovemaking session and she wasn't fool enough to mistake it for anything more.

Nick lowered two loaded plates onto the table and poured green tea from a pot into his cup. He sipped it and looked out over the vista beyond the windows washed clean by the rain. His heart was full to bursting with smiles and joy. The grass seemed more vibrant, the sky more striking, the sun more glowing. It was like the world had been created afresh. Like he was a new man. Whole and hearty. He tucked into his food with an appetite he hadn't felt since he was a kid and when Emily settled into the seat across from him, her hair mussed from sleep, her lips a warm temptation, her smile, soothing, he stopped mid-movement to savour the moment.

"What?" she grumbled and reached for her knife and fork. She ate like a woman starved and he laughed. They'd both worked up an appetite and when she wiped her mouth clean on a serviette and reached for her tea, she looked sated and satisfied.

"Good?"

"Better than good."

He hoped they were talking about more than the breakfast he'd whipped up, his body buzzing with energy. She'd stoked a fire in his blood. She'd stirred him into caring. She'd ruined him for any other woman. "Are you ready to head for home?"

"My clothes are dry," she said, testing them where they hung in front of the fire. "I'll go and get changed. Thanks for the loan of yours."

"I kind of like you in my clothes." He couldn't keep the burr from his tone.

"I kind of like me in your clothes, too." She smiled, and he felt it like a warm wave all the way to his toes. A wave that lifted his spirits until they soared over the paddocks and the sea like a wayward bird.

"I'm not sure I can keep our night together from being written all over my face. You've taken a broken man and made him feel whole. Your forgiveness means everything."

"It's not my forgiveness you need." Her movement stopped and that doe-like gaze of hers settled on his, warm and luscious.

"It's your own."

"I don't think I'll ever be able to forgive myself. My wife died. *My child.*" His words cut off like someone had spliced his throat. Like a blade was stuck there for the foreseeable future. "That's not something I can forgive, but for now…" He looked out to the horizon. "I hope I can move forward."

"It was an accident. You did everything you could." Emily's chocolate gaze burned into his before flitting to the window and then down to the table. She fidgeted, her grip on her clothing tight enough to strangle, her shoulders rounding as if she carried a burden that was too heavy or too cumbersome.

"What is it?" His skin tightened and a chill wormed its way down his spine. He watched her internal battle, the shadows that darkened her eyes, the tension around her mouth, the crease in her forehead. Would she trust him enough to tell him or would she keep whatever it was to herself? He couldn't breathe. He couldn't move. He wanted her trust. He wanted it more than he'd wanted her body. This was an attraction that shook him to the core.

"The baby…" Her gaze snagged on his, liquid and soft, and he saw the moment she surrendered, the relief that washed through her.

"…it wasn't yours, Nick. I'm sorry." Her voice was tender, like he was made of eggshells and might crack. "Charliese had a paternity test done. It was one of the reasons she wanted a divorce."

The blade in his throat twisted and caught like a barb. His stomach knotted and clenched. His muscles banded and a sheen of sweat formed on his brow. The baby wasn't his.

His wife had been pregnant with another man's child. The knowledge sat heavy in his gut. How unhappy must she have been? How lonely? Shame burned in his veins. Enough to seek connection with a man outside of their marriage.

He'd killed a child. But he hadn't killed *his* child. The sting, the piercing throb that had gouged his insides since he'd stood alone at the cemetery was still there, but the fist inside his belly unfurled. A bit. Enough for him to draw breath without pain. "It shouldn't change anything, but it does." Tears welled in his eyes and his vision blurred. "Thank you. It's more than I deserve. *You* are more than I deserve."

"I blamed you even though I knew the accident was put down to the condition of the road and the weather." Her shoulders slumped forward. "You weren't drunk. You weren't careless, but I blamed you anyway. I held you responsible because you survived, and she didn't. I blamed you because she was unhappy. I was wrong to do that. Relationships are complex."

"Yes."

He moved over to where she stood with her clothes in her hands and took her beautiful face in his. "Thank you, Em. What I feel for you right now feels like nothing I've felt before."

"We're on a post-coital high, Wheatley. I don't trust a word you say, but I thank you for the sentiment. And I loved our night together. It was very special."

"You're a true cynic."

"I am." She smiled. "And I value our friendship. Enough to break Charliese's confidence, but I think given the circumstances, she would have wanted me to tell you. I need to get changed. You'd better get me back to my people."

"I like your people." And he liked her. He was attracted to her, but he wasn't the man he used to be. This wasn't a skin-deep kind of attraction. This was a long-haul, I-want-this-woman-in-my-life kind of attraction. But he didn't trust himself to say it and he knew she wasn't ready to hear it. What they'd shared went way, way beyond a physical connection. This was no flash of lightning in a stormy sky. The connection he felt with Emily had roots that went deep. As deep as the land. As deep as the ocean.

She was home-and-hearth perfect and filled the gaping holes inside him. But for once, his needs were not at the top of his mind. She was no Charliese, easily swept away by love… and just as easily swept away by the love of another man. Emily needed time to adjust to the idea. Like sowing a seed, he needed to nurture its growth. It needed time to develop. He'd learned a lot from nature, and he wasn't going to mess this up. He planned to convince her—through actions *and* words—that he was worth the risk.

Chapter Eight

Emily kissed Nick farewell at the gate to the While Away B&B. It was a slow, soft, simmering kiss that spoke of feelings. Feelings that were too new, too fresh, too pristine to put into words. He wanted to hold on to her and never let her go, but Carmie was running towards them and he had to pull himself together. There was more at stake than just the two of them and he realised it then. They came as a package deal and it was a package he liked.

"E-Em. Nick."

Emily took Carmie in her arms and hugged her, her gaze on Nick's over Carmie's head. He knew what she was thinking. He could have recited it word for word. This is what's important to me. More important than any man. And his own gaze didn't falter. He promised to love them both. But he saw the scepticism in her gaze. The lack of trust. The pulling back. The disconnection. The sadness before she smiled and bantered with Carmie as if she didn't have a care in the world. It was then his gaze shifted to the veranda and he saw the figure that lingered there like Satan or he-who-shall-not-be-named. Waiting. A chill crawled over his skin and down his spine like a thousand tiny feet, a marching battalion.

Phillip wasn't worthy of her.

Hell, *he* wasn't worthy of her, but he was a damn sight more worthy than Phillip. And it was then he decided he wasn't in a hurry to leave.

"Nick, let's play a game." Carmie rushed towards him and wrapped her arms around his waist.

"How can a man say, no, when you ask like that?" He grinned at her. "Come on, then. Do your worst."

"I'm gonna beat you," she declared.

"You don't have a chance."

"Yes, I do. Come on." She grabbed his hand and dragged him towards the house. He glanced back at Emily and winked. Her smile warmed him like a winter's hearth, but there was worry in her eyes. The lay of the land had changed between them and he could see how unsettled she felt. He was kind of unsettled himself. It was like they'd hit the real world at cosmic speed and the impact was dizzying.

"Morning, Phillip," Nick said. The fellow recoiled like he'd been slapped. Had he recognised the elation in Nick's tone? The morning-after glow was hard to disguise and what glowed inside of him had the power of the sun. "That was some storm last night."

Phillip's eyes narrowed as if he knew Nick wasn't talking about the weather. Perceptive of him. Or maybe he was just the suspicious kind. No doubt, he would have taken advantage of the situation, but that wasn't how it happened, and Nick wasn't going to entertain the vision of their night together through the filter of Phillip's eyes. It wasn't a one-night lust-fest. It wasn't a cheap and tacky kind of seduction. Nick pushed back with his eyes. *You know nothing about Emily. She's not the woman you think she is. She's more. So much more.* And the irony was that Phillip didn't know Emily could see him. The real him.

The snake that slithered behind the handsome eyes. And Nick could see him, too. The old Nick would have been impressed by the flashy money and the gloss. The new Nick was far from impressed and he wanted the fellow gone.

"Come on, Nick." Carmie pulled at him. He hadn't realised he stood with his feet wide, in fighting stance, facing off with Phillip.

"Bring it on, sweet cheeks." He looked over his shoulder and observed Phillip's attention shift to Emily. *Bring it on, mate, if you think you have a chance with Em.* He wanted to stay and defend his turf. He wanted to wrestle the guy down, bundle him up and dump him back in his helicopter. He wanted to warn Emily. But he didn't need to. She saw through Phillip. He had to trust her to make her own decisions. It wasn't easy. His muscles tightened and knotted and banded in his neck as he followed Carmie. He had to trust Emily with his heart. The same way he wanted her to trust him. And for a moment, fear took his other hand.

Emily didn't want a relationship... with any man. And not because of the state of his face or his bank account, but because she didn't trust him not to leave her. And then Nick realised what she probably didn't realise herself. Emily used Carmie as a shield. Even if she didn't have Carmie to consider, she would push men away. She didn't trust a man to love her. She thought she wasn't worthy of love. She feared a man would leave.

And that's when he turned into the kitchen and his world shattered like he'd walked into a pane of glass, the shards lodging in his chest. Spread across the kitchen table were A4-sized glossy photos of Emily.

Photos of magazine covers—Harper's BAZAAR and Elle and

Vogue—with her face on the front. She wasn't just a model…
she was a top tier model and the reality of it hit him like a
tsunami, swamping his hopes and his plans. He couldn't get air
into his punctured lungs. He remembered her words and they
ate into his heart like acid. She wanted to be a Victoria's Secret
Angel. She wouldn't stay here for long, and that's what Phillip
hoped to remind her. She was too sought after, her career too
hot to dally in a backwater like French Island for any longer
than it took to find a new carer for Carmie and her mum. How
long would she make this kind of money? How long would her
career fly so high?

Not long enough for her to linger here. There wasn't room
in her life for a relationship with him. Nick's heart twisted like
a kite plunging towards the earth. Gone was the wind that had
lifted it and danced with it and brought its Ramin dowel and
cloth to life.

He settled himself beside Carmie and, like the first-class
actor he used to be, he plastered a makeshift smile on his face
and forced himself to act. To act like he hadn't hoped. To act
like his dreams—still fresh and new like the green shoots Joey
loved to eat—hadn't shattered around him. To act like he was
solid instead of hollow.

Phillip came into the room, his face smug. He knew what
Nick should have known from the outset. He couldn't leave
his farm. He wouldn't leave his farm. There wasn't a chance
he'd follow Emily into her world. He shunned the spotlight.
He'd turned his back on fame and judgement. He'd chosen to
hide his face, unlike Emily, whose face was her world. It was a
clever reminder. A death blow.

He settled down to play a game with the gorgeously imperfect
girl he adored. He may belong here, but Emily didn't. When

had he forgotten the bleeding obvious? When had he fooled himself into thinking she'd be happy baking in his kitchen, working on his land, and saving his calves from their own stupidity?

He was a man drowned. And there was no way to reach the light of day.

Emily tidied the photos into a pile and dropped them onto a chair. She went through the motions of making tea while Phillip hovered nearby. She felt his presence like a lead weight. Why had he left the photos there? To remind Nick—and her—who she was? She couldn't have Nick *and* her career. She couldn't stay here and play happy families forever. She had work to do. She had a living to make. She needed to get back to her world, before the pain of leaving became too unbearable. Already, she ached to stay. Already, the call of her career was scarcely audible. Phillip was right to remind her. She couldn't pursue a relationship with Nick or stay here with her family forever. She needed to find a manager for While Away, and a carer for her mum and Carmie. And she needed to get back to work.

Her work was far from a hardship.

Her work was glamorous and wonderful and full of men like Phillip. Men she could never love. Unlike Nick, who had touched her deeply enough for her to want—truly want—what she could have with him. He was real and grounded and rooted in the earth her grandparents had thrived on. He'd suffered. He'd grown. He was far from the man who'd failed her friend. Maybe with him she could find a love like the one her grandparents had shared. Her thoughts spun with wishes, but the fact remained that she had to leave. And soon before she lost sight of what was important.

She lowered the tea things onto the table. "I need to see Mum."

Phillip settled himself at the table and nodded. He lifted the pot and poured a cup. He was a good-looking guy and he knew it. Wealthy, confident, and out of place sitting at their kitchen table. He didn't fit in with her life here and his presence was a warning call. She needed to go back. Her phone had multiple missed calls. All from her agent. And a text message from the company she'd hired to find her a new manager, confirming their scheduled interviews for Tuesday at ten o'clock.

She wanted to dump it in the ocean.

She wanted Phillip to leave and take his reminders of their glossy world with him.

She wanted to stay. She wanted to be with Nick. She wanted a love like her grandparents had shared.

Except she couldn't. Even the thought brought a cold sweat to her brow. Nick couldn't save her. No man could. Love was an illusion, like the woman on those magazine covers. She wasn't real. She was staged. A trick of lighting and makeup. The real woman was the woman who cared for those she loved. And that was enough. That was more than enough.

Emily picked up the tea she'd made for her mum and left without a backward glance. She could sense the tension between Nick and Phillip. Like two outraged cocks in a fighting pit, waiting to tear each other's heads off. She didn't belong to either one of them. There was nothing for them to fight over.

"Hi, Mum. How are you feeling?" She lowered the tea to the bedside table and helped her mum to sit up. She opened the blinds a smidge to let in some light.

"Better now that you're here."

Emily straightened the bedclothes and settled herself on the bed. "Did Phillip look after you?"

"He was very charming, but he's old enough to be your father, Em."

"Not many ten-year-old boys have babies." Her insides churned, and her skin heated and flushed. Why did she feel like a teenager who would never be good enough?

"He acts older than thirty-five."

"He has a very healthy ego. It comes from being wealthy and powerful."

"Do you love him?" Her mother's gaze flicked away and back. Her eyes were the same colour as Emily's, but dull and muddied and distant like the cold murk of the dam.

"No. I told him it wouldn't work out between us. He came to change my mind, but he's only confirmed what I already knew. He doesn't know me at all."

"You keep men at a distance, honey. Don't let my experience with your father ruin your life." She took a sip of her tea. "There are good men out there. Your grandfather was a good man. I thought your father was a good man. Perhaps he was, but he couldn't handle the reality of your sister's condition. He felt responsible."

"Mum, he left us, never to be heard from again." She took a deep breath of the stale air. "I don't want to leave, but I can't stay much longer. I need to earn enough money to keep us going for the rest of our lives. I need to keep the big picture in mind. I have interviews for a new manager/carer on Tuesday." She had to toughen up and do what needed to be done. She had responsibilities. She couldn't afford to soften. She couldn't afford to entertain the whimsy of sharing the load. The load was hers to carry. Alone.

"I've seen how Nick looks at you. He's a wealthy man. You could marry him and then you wouldn't need to work, and you wouldn't need to leave us. Better still, you'd live on your grandparents' land." The thought shone in her eyes like light on broken glass.

"I don't want to rely on a man for our financial well-being." She didn't want to rely on a man, full stop.

"Phillip showed me photos of your work. He printed them for me. You look gorgeous, but he explained how competitive it is in the modelling world. How risky it is to step out for even a short time. He said there are beautiful girls lined up to take your place. It sounds cut-throat and stressful."

"I can handle the pressure, Mum." Unlike you. Emily crushed the toxic thought. She couldn't fall apart. Someone had to function. "This is temporary. You'll feel better soon. You'll get back to your painting and the business and looking after Carmie, but we still need someone to help."

"I wish you could stay, love."

"I wish I could, too." And a big part of her did want to stay. But not the part that worried about food and money and bills. "I need to work and that means travel. I have to go where the work is. I'll come back as often as I can." She wouldn't let her mum guilt her into abandoning her career. Not when she'd gone hungry because there wasn't enough money for food. Not when she'd had to tell Carmie they would eat tomorrow and think, hopefully. She liked seeing Carmie in nice clothes. She liked knowing they were warm and well looked after. She liked the security that came from earning a good income. And she had a window of time to prepare for the future.

"Don't let it suck you dry. I wouldn't wish this illness

on anyone, least of all you. Thank you for coming home." She held Emily's gaze, chocolate brown to chocolate brown. "Home is where your heart is, honey. This island. This small community."

"My heart is in my chest. It goes where I go." And she wasn't foolish enough to trust it to anyone. Man *or* woman. "I can't earn my kind of income here."

"I know. But we miss you when you're gone."

"I miss you, too." Simply said, yet the words left a gaping wound in her chest. "You and Carmie are my first priorities. Always."

"Thanks for the tea. You need to get back to your guests. I love you, honey."

"Okay, Mum. I love you, too." It was a love that hurt. A dull ache in her chest. Emily picked up the empty cup and kissed her mum on the forehead before she lowered the blind and shut out the light. She stopped at the doorway to observe the still mound under the covers. This was what she was determined to avoid. No man would bring her to this. No man would take her energy and leave her broken. It was a good reminder. A timely reminder. What she felt for Nick was too dangerous. Too risky. She needed to get back to work, where she felt safe. The Phillips of the world were easy to deflect. The Nicks? Not so much.

Emily sat at the table with Phillip and sipped her tea. Nick and Carmie came over to join them, their game finished. Carmie's effervescence would never grow old and she kept the conversation light-hearted and fun. Emily would miss her, and the man who carefully observed her from the other side of the table. Questions lurked in his eyes—questions and concerns. She doused the flare of hope. There was no way to reconcile their separate worlds. She'd lost her mind. She got the feeling he could see her. Truly see her. The woman behind the face. And it was disconcerting.

Emily turned to Phillip. "What time are you planning to leave today?"

"This afternoon," he said. "I can come back for you in a few days if you'd like. When is the new carer due to start?"

"I won't know until after Tuesday. Hopefully, straight away. Thank you for the offer, but I'm fine. I have a flight booked next weekend."

"Where are you off to?" Nick asked. His tone was bright—too bright—as if gilded by sheer determination. As if he didn't care, when every taut, rigid muscle in his body told her he did.

She didn't want him to care. She was used to being the car*er*, not the car*ee*, although she knew her mum and sister loved her. "I'm due in Milan next Monday." There was *I'm sorry* in her tone for she should never have slept with him. It wasn't fair. She'd given him hope where there was none. She'd allowed him to think she cared about him—and hell, she did. She'd lost her mind in his arms, and somehow, he'd slipped under her radar and into her heart. Every pain that shadowed his eyes hit her like a dart. Every thought that creased his forehead sent an answering twinge to her own. Every movement that stirred the air sent an answering pulse to that part of her that craved him still. Her muscle memory needed little encouragement to send it into overdrive. The air between them zapped with nonverbal communication and her body throbbed with all that they'd shared. A muscle ticked on the good side of his face as if his lopsided smile took a superhuman effort. Never had she experienced anything like this—her body hungered and yearned for his touch. Never had she wanted a man more. Never had she found it so difficult to harden her heart.

But harden it she must.

"How long will you be gone?" His tone was interested and curious, and she got the clear message he wouldn't stop her.

"A few weeks at the most."

"Where to after Milan?"

"Paris for a week, then New York. I'll be back after that to make sure the new carer is working out."

"I can keep an eye on things while you're gone." His inflection was casual, his words easy, but his blue gaze was piercing.

"That would be great, thank you."

Phillip wrapped his arm around the back of her chair, and she stiffened. The attraction she'd felt for him was gone. Gone with his insensitivity towards Carmie and Joey. Gone with his rudeness to Nick, his impatience with the demands of her family. He didn't love her. He loved the kudos of a model on his arm and his needs were transparent.

Nick relaxed back in his seat and smiled. He must have seen the way she recoiled. He read her with ease. Phillip wasn't a threat.

"Are you planning to whisk Em away for a nice lunch somewhere today?" he asked casually as if he didn't care, but Emily knew better.

"No. We'll keep that for Milan." Nick contracted in the middle like he'd been physically struck. He wasn't a part of her world and Phillip was.

"We won't have time for a nice lunch in Milan," she said. "We'll be working long hours and I'm not there for a holiday." She stood and carried her cup over to the sink. "Would anyone like another tea?"

"No, thanks. I need to get going. There's work to do after the storm. Fences to check and I need to see how our little friend is faring today."

"I'll walk you out."

"That would be lovely."

Emily ignored Phillip's dark glare. It wasn't like they were dating. He'd arrived uninvited. He had no reason to feel he had any proprietary rights over her. He was an ex- at best, if someone could be an ex- after five unofficial dates. He hadn't respected her decision to end their relationship. He'd lied to inveigle his way into her home and her private life. She wasn't feeling particularly warm towards him.

"That man makes my skin crawl. Are you sure you're safe around him? You have my number."

"Is that your way of asking me to call you?"

"It's my way of looking after those I care about, and I do care about you, Em. I know it's early days and I don't know how this can work when you're out of the country more often than you're here. I know I don't fit into your professional world. I don't want to, but I'm happy to share this world with you. When you're home."

Where was the possessive egotist Charliese had described? This man offered her the open sky with open arms and an open heart. No attempt to entrap or ensnare her. No selfish agenda. "I don't know how often I'll be here."

"I'm not going anywhere."

He was solid, like the rock embedded beneath their feet. Below the grass. Below the soil. They stopped at the gate, his mud-splashed vehicle on the other side. He took her face in his hands and kissed her slowly and her toes curled inside her boots. "I see you, Em. And I like what I see."

"I see you, too, and I like what I see, but it doesn't change the facts."

"I'll keep your people safe while you're gone."

"I'd appreciate that." Tears burned in her eyes and she cursed, swiping them away.

"I'd like to see you again before you go. We could do dinner on Tuesday night at my place if you like. I'll cook."

"Like a date?"

"No. Not like a date. Like a home-cooked meal with a guy whose feelings for you are more than neighbourly. I'd like to hear how the interviews go."

"Okay. Sure." And there was no way they'd end up in bed again. Lesson learned.

Emily rolled over and studied the man beside her. He'd changed her in ways she didn't dare reflect upon. She'd hungered for him. Hungered. She'd never hungered for a man before. Not like this. The moon shone in from the window and the outline of his face was handsome. A straight blade of a nose, square jaw, and thick, healthy hair. But it was his smile that lifted his face from merely handsome to stunning—slightly lopsided with the tightness of his skin on the damaged side—but to her, magical. And his eyes were electric blue in his tanned face. He saw only the scar that marred his cheek, but she saw everything else. The gentle kindness that shone in his eyes when he spoke of Carmie, the humour that shifted the violet shadows, the desire that brewed there when he looked at her. They'd made it through dinner... just.

Until she'd lowered her cutlery and what seethed and stormed and smouldered between them couldn't be denied. His touch was addictive and heady and delicious. She knew the pheromone effect and right now, hers were rampaging. What burned in her breast was fanciful, but it seemed real. Her skin was alive with the aftermath of his touch. She breathed him in and his musky scent filled her head with crazy wishes. Like wishing she could wake up beside him every morning. Like wishing she could stay here, in their private paradise. Like wishing she could throw away all that she'd worked so hard to achieve because compared to being here—right here—it seemed insignificant.

Could it work for them? A life together was based on more than a night or two of mind-blowing sex. She couldn't give up the security of her job. She couldn't trust that he wouldn't lose interest or decide Carmie was an imposition. This was attraction. Pure and powerful. A few more days and she'd be gone. She had a fabulous new carer, Sasha. A young woman who planned to move to the island. Carmie would love her. She was a few years younger than Emily and spoke of opportunities for Carmie to spend time with others who have Down syndrome.

There was no way around the gaping distance between their worlds. Nick couldn't leave his stock or his land, which he tended so carefully. And she couldn't risk leaving her job. Not when her family's future depended on her, and her career gave her everything she'd promised herself. Financial security. Independence. Travel. She couldn't entrust her family's safety and their well-being to anyone else. *Her* safety and well-being. Better to stand strong and alone than to risk everything.

He would let her go. She knew he would. He wouldn't stop her, and the thought left a tear in the fabric of her soul.

Somewhere in the long night, Nick reached out and they made love again, so tender it brought tears to her eyes. They lay tangled together, his breath slowing to a steady ebb and flow against her neck. She knew she was in danger, for this man touched her like no other. Deeply and irrevocably.

Emily stood on the deck of the ferry and watched the Tankerton Jetty become smaller and smaller. The motor hummed and throbbed beneath her feet, the sound of the water a steady, rhythmic splash as the vessel sliced through the choppy waves. The wind pushed and pulled like the words inside her head. Go. Stay. Want to go. Want to stay. Need to go. Need to stay. A single, dark-coated figure stood against the steely grey of the sky and her eyes couldn't leave him. She watched him until he became a miniscule black dot and the pain in her chest crystallised into a fierce point so sharp it arrowed into her heart and lodged there.

Carmie's tear-drenched face was etched into the back of her eyelids and her mother's resigned sigh echoed in her ears. It hurt to leave. And this time the hurt near blasted a hole right through her.

Going home was difficult, like birth or death. She'd learned to loathe the ferry ride. Her phone buzzed inside her pocket and she dragged it out.

I miss you already.

I miss you, too... she typed with shaking fingers, the few letters taking the work of fifty by the time she'd deleted the wrong ones and retyped the right ones. She blamed the rocking movement of the boat and the flat, grey light that made the screen near impossible to read. She wasn't one for sentimental nonsense and she dropped the phone back into her pocket. Where was the clean break she preferred? She'd told him not to write. He'd said he would. She'd told him a long-distance relationship would never work. He'd told her, she'd never tried one with him. She'd told him she knew better. He'd told her, he knew best. He was pig-headed and stubborn and a whole host of other character flaws. But he'd gotten under her skin, like the rust that festered beneath the thick paint on the rail beneath her hand.

He'd tried to save Charliese. Emily hadn't known that. It changed everything, and nothing. He hadn't just saved himself. He'd tried to save Charliese. He tried to save her every night in his sleep.

What if *she* had only weeks to live? Where would she want to be? Travelling the world alone or with her family and Nick on the farm? She loved her work and once she broke the connection to home, she'd get on with doing what she did well. But this time, the connection was more like an umbilical cord carrying oxygen and life-sustaining nutrients, and the disconnection was more like death. Like part of her wilted. Like the arrow point in her chest burned a hole. Like every breath was a razor blade to her throat. Every minute an eternity.

She went through the motions. She got herself to the airport. She sat through the endless flight. She ate, but she was a shadow of herself. A spectre, for her substance wasn't there. She felt splintered. Separated and isolated from those around her. Voices were a mere sound from a long way off. Faces and smiles were a visage before her eyes. And she fought the desire to curl up in a bed in a darkened room and pull the covers over her head. Never would she surrender. Her scars ran deep and maybe that was why she'd connected with Nick. They'd both been hurt by life. But she chose to function. She chose to put one foot in front of the other and strut down the catwalk, her chin high, her smile serene, her heart not so much.

Chapter Nine

Nick eyed the small array of people in front of him at the church hall in Cranbourne on the mainland. Carmie stood front and centre, her smile wider than the rest. Who knew she'd love acting so much? "We have six weeks until this film is a wrap. We can do this. You're doing a brilliant job."

"Yes," Carmie cried. "Yes, Nick. We can."

"Yes," the group chorused with slurred s's.

"Then let's take it from the top."

Carmie moved onto the set, her hair pulled back in a ponytail with a pink scarf around her neck, a full pink skirt, and a black top. The story was about four girls who worked in a café in the fifties and the relationships they developed. Nick kept the action moving. Short scenes. Short lines. The set looked great with its black and white linoleum floor and a cool retro coffee machine and milkshake maker. It was *Happy Days* with a twist... literally and the kids loved it. Twist and shout and let it all out. And they practiced. Oh, they practiced every day. Never had he seen such a committed group of actors. They loved the dancing. They loved the singing. And he couldn't have guessed he'd get so much joy from the directing.

He'd thought his Hollywood days were over. Maybe they

were. But he was getting interest in his scripts. A lot of interest in his scripts. Until now, he'd said no to every directing opportunity except this one. This one was irresistible. Carmie was irresistible when she was on a mission. And she'd wanted his help. He settled himself behind the camera and counted them in. Their costumes looked terrific. Their makeup looked subtle, but glamorous, thanks to Sasha. He eyed the red-haired woman at his side in her denim shorts and summer top. She mimed the parts. Demonstrated the moves. She was a powerhouse of energy.

He was glad for the distraction. It spared him from the emptiness in his home. The silence that settled around him the minute he walked in. He'd never worked so hard. He worked until he was so physically tired, he couldn't fight the pull of sleep. The sensory memory of Emily nestled against him kept the nightmares at bay and with sleep, he healed. With sleep, he coped. Still, his survivor-guilt burned inside him like a thousand fires. He felt the presence of that child-soul beside him when he worked. He'd taken to talking to her. And he'd decided he wanted a child with Emily the moment she was done with her career... the moment she was ready... if she still wanted him. And if she was worried about Carmie's rogue chromosome, he wasn't. Carmie and her friends had taught him a great deal about happiness. About accepting his flaws and his faults and his scars, and he was grateful for the lesson.

He'd tried to keep Charliese to himself, like a sweaty palm closed around a violet or a butterfly, the sheer act of impris-onment enough to crush the life out of whatever love they'd shared. He knew now that love, true love, grew from trust and faith and patience, and it was like technicolour after black and white. It couldn't be stolen. It couldn't be corralled. It needed to breathe. It needed to spread its wings and be free.

"Okay, last time through this scene and we'll call it quits for today. I think Sasha has ice cream standing by."

"Yay." The whole group stampeded for the small kitchenette at the side of the hall and he chuckled. He'd forgotten. Don't mention ice cream until after the work was done or the work was done. His phone pinged and he grappled for it.

"Okay. We'll take five!" He spoke to an empty room.

Can you chat?

Emily. His fingers shook as he punched in the numbers, his movements so rushed, he fumbled and had to start again. His heart pounded in his chest, and his stomach surged and pitched like the ferry on a wintry Western Port Bay. But the weather was fine. Better than fine and he couldn't stop the grin. "Hey, Em."

"Hey back at you. What are you up to?"

"Rehearsal. Your sister loves the limelight. Six weeks and it'll be a wrap." He held the phone close to his ear like he'd entered a sanctuary or a cocoon. A quiet place where there was just him and Em. Her voice loosened the knots in his body. Knots he hadn't known were there until they weren't.

"You're incredible."

His chest swelled. "You know it was Sasha who started this group with Carmie, right?"

"Yes, but it's you who has taken them on the most amazing journey."

"They are the amazing ones. I'm just a conduit and quite frankly, they've taught me a lot."

"I still love you for doing it."

If that's all it took to make her love him, he'd create films for Carmie and her Downs friends for the rest of his days.

"I'm glad to hear it. How's Hawaii going?" He settled himself on the buffed wooden boards of the floor. Air blew across his forehead, stirred by the metal blades of a pedestal fan, cool against the fine sheen of perspiration. The sun pushed through the stained-glass windows creating a rainbow of dappled colour and the ceiling soared above him with exposed wooden beams. It was a holy place. Holier now with Em's voice in his ear.

"Warm. The weather's perfect here all year round."

Her voice washed over him like a caress. "One week and counting, Stone. I'm looking forward to seeing you again." Who was he kidding? He was counting the minutes and the seconds.

"I can't wait to see you either."

"The weather's been scorching, and the B&B is booked through to the end of March. Carmie has been helping Marge out at the general store and she's busy at The Beez Kneez."

"Sasha tells me you opened the café about a decade ago. You never said."

"Facilitated. Funded. That's all. A friend of mine suffered a serious brain injury when he came off his motorbike and he couldn't get a job. I figured I could help him out. But I helped from a distance. It wasn't until recently I got more hands-on. Carmie is a huge asset by the way."

"I owe you so much."

"You don't owe me anything. Except a visit. I'm a lonely man. And Christmas was eight weeks ago."

Emily lowered the phone and stared across the rose-tipped waves. The sand was soft and silky beneath her feet. The sun was a raging ball of fire in the sky, hanging on to the day by a thread. She hadn't envisaged having a child. Ever. Her stomach stirred with panic. And nausea. She'd spent the best part of the morning throwing up and she hadn't been able to look at food for days. Her stomach was still flat, but it wouldn't be long until people would know. The shoot that afternoon had exhausted her, and she'd napped for an hour before heading out to Waikiki beach to clear her head.

Lost in her own thoughts, she didn't hear Phillip come up behind her.

"Don't move," he said.

Emily was slow to pull herself out of her reverie and sensed rather than heard the rally of clicks. She turned and Phillip stood before her, tanned and fit in a white shirt and ripped jeans, wet around the bottom like he'd walked through the shallows. He'd dropped his brown loafers on the sand and his feet were bare. His camera was around his neck. "Hi," she said.

"You make a lovely picture silhouetted against the sunset. These will be gorgeous."

"Thanks." Being gorgeous was a blessing and a curse.

"I missed you at the hotel. The others are at the bar." He raked a hand through his hair. "The Victoria's Secret shoot last week went well. Very well. I just heard from your agent. She said you weren't answering your phone." He kissed her cheek and stood back to observe her. "You look pale, my dear. Are you okay?"

The citrusy spice of his aftershave pulled at the back of her throat, too pungent, too cloying. Her sense of smell was on steroids. "I'm fine. Thanks. I needed some quiet time. It was a long day." She turned her gaze to the horizon and took a deep breath of the briny air.

"I hope you're not coming down with something." His tone

was warm, concerned. They'd found their way back to a comfortable place and she was grateful for his friendship.

"No. I don't think so."

"Kresley said I could tell you the good news. You did it. We did it. You've been offered a contract by Victoria's Secret…"

"Are you serious?" Elation burst through her like a firework. A firework snuffed by thick, stormy cloud.

"Let's just say I put in a good word where it counts. We have a meeting—the day after tomorrow—in Ohio. It would mean living in the US for the duration of the contract, which is yet to be negotiated. Exclusivity, except for an arrangement between Victoria's Secret and *Glamour Magazine*. This is your chance to make it big. Bigger than big. Huge." He sat back with smug satisfaction.

"I don't know what to say." She should be ecstatic. She should be leaping around like she'd won the lottery. She should be throwing herself in Phillip's arms and kissing him until he cried for mercy. This was everything she'd dreamed of. This was everything she'd worked for. Everything she wanted was hers for the taking. Instead, her body was slow-witted and still. Her mind grappled for traction. "I can't thank you enough." Her gaze shifted from his triumphant one to the pink glow on the horizon. Twilight was moving in, like a thick violet curtain. "I've wanted to be a Victoria's Secret Angel since I was a teenager." Her tone was wistful. Ohio might as well be in another galaxy.

"I know it." His gaze drew hers. "So, what's wrong. Why aren't you thrilled?"

"I am thrilled. I'm just overwhelmed." She fought to smile, but it was a battle she lost. "It's the most amazing opportunity."

"I thought you'd be ecstatic. Those don't look like happy

tears."

And now she'd hurt him. "I can't thank you enough."

"I care for you, my dear. Deeply."

His gaze intensified and a warning shimmied along Emily's spine. She took a long, bolstering breath, trying to calm the choppy sensation in her stomach.

"I want you to know how much." He got down on his knees and fumbled in his pocket for a velvet box, which he pulled open and held open for her. A square diamond the size of a quail egg on a white gold band nestled inside. "Please, make me the happiest man alive and agree to marry me. You know I love you. And these past few months we've become friends. Good friends. I want to make you happy. I want to give you the world. And I get it now. Anything less than marriage is not enough."

Emily gazed into his handsome face, tinged with colour from the setting sun. Her blood pressure spiked, a loud gush in her ears. Her chest hurt. Her heart pounded. He thought she'd held out because she wanted marriage? She dragged air into her stupefied lungs. "Thank you for caring about me. You know how much I value our friendship."

"We're good together, my dear. With me, your career will be amazing. I'll open doors you haven't seen yet. I'll take you to the highest echelon." He looked up at her, his eyes sparkling with dreams and hopes and whimsy.

Emily's skin prickled like a cold breeze had come off the water, except the evening was balmy and warm and still. *Don't marry me and your career won't be amazing?* "Phillip, thank you. I'm flattered and blessed that you care enough to ask and I'm grateful for everything you've done for me." She lowered herself down to her knees and reached out to cup his cheek, the dark stubbly growth prickly against her palm. "I don't want to lose your friendship and I don't want to hurt you, but I can't marry you. I'm sorry."

He closed the box and put it back inside his pocket. He sat back on his heels and his shoulders curled forwards like his camera suddenly weighed more than he could bear.

"I've carried this ring with me since I came to French Island. I thought we were good together. I thought you wanted me as much as I wanted you... until I saw you with the farmer. It's him isn't it? You can't love me because you love him. His Hollywood days are over. He lives a mediocre life in the middle of nowhere. What does he have to offer you? Nothing but washed-up dreams."

His words pierced her heart to the raw softness inside. She did indeed love the farmer and it scared her to bits. "I'm not free to love any man. I need to look after Carmie for the rest of her life. And my mum. My family is the most important thing to me."

"They have a carer. You don't have to sacrifice your life for your family."

"I don't see it as a sacrifice."

He took her hands in his. "Emily, please, don't throw away this opportunity out of some misguided sense of guilt. You can't live your life for them. Your life is your own."

"No, it isn't." Emily turned back to the horizon, where the sun had lost its battle and disappeared, leaving a wash of pink and orange and purple that was slowly being devoured by the night. Tears welled in her eyes and she took sharp gulps of air. She fanned her face with her hand. She had to be strong. She had to hold it together. She had to remember what was important. "I can't go to Ohio. I'm sorry." Emily fought the desire to twist her fingers together, to bow her head, to turn away, but pride made her lift her chin, her gaze steady on Phillip's. "I need to go home. Something urgent has come up."

"This is a once-in-a-lifetime opportunity." Phillip's face near contorted with frustration. "Your family is like ballast dragging you down. You could soar, Emily. You could soar to the damn heavens and make enough money to pay for an army of carers."

"I know." Her heart laboured like concrete ran in her veins. "It's everything I've dreamed of."

"Then why don't you grasp it with both hands?"

His glare near razed the flesh from her bones and tears welled in her eyes. Scorching. Blinding. Burning.

"I'm pregnant." Her voice was a whisper, a barely there scrap of sound. She shifted her gaze to the darkening sky and missed Phillip's reaction. She didn't want to see it. She felt like a fool. Like a rookie teenager who should have known better.

"You can't be serious. You're serious?" He didn't speak for a full five minutes and she couldn't muster her own voice to shatter the silence. Tears spilled down her cheeks and she swiped them away.

"What are you going to do?"

"I don't know yet."

"The fact that you don't know tells me you want to keep it. You're going to throw everything away? Your dreams? Everything you've worked for? I don't see the father of this baby rushing to your aid."

"He doesn't know."

"It's the farmer, isn't it? I knew it. I should throttle that lowlife. He's ruined your career. He did this on purpose. It was the only way to keep you on that island."

Emily didn't speak. She couldn't. The words were tangled in

the monster-sized swell that rose in her throat like a Big Wave. Had Nick done this on purpose? No. She wouldn't believe it of him. She'd trusted him. He'd given her the freedom to come and go as she pleased. He'd shown none of the possessiveness that Charliese had complained of. Because he'd plotted to get her pregnant? Because he knew her well enough to know she would choose to keep a baby?

"This changes everything. Or nothing. You don't have to go through with the pregnancy. You don't have to do this. The timing couldn't be worse."

"I know." The wave crested and fresh tears welled in her eyes. Her vision blurred. She cried for her career. For her life as she knew it. For her relationship with Nick. Not because she thought he was capable of engineering this—although the thought lingered like an oil slick in her mind—but because he was the kind of man who would do the right thing and ask her to marry him. And she'd have to say no, when she might have said yes if their feelings had been free to grow without a ticking clock. She wanted the fairy tale. She wanted love.

She wanted this baby. Even if it shared Carmie's disability. She was a fierce mama bear. She could deal with this. She didn't need Nick's help or Phillip's help or anyone else's help and somehow, she would manage. She always did.

"I'll reschedule the meeting in Ohio. Take a week to figure out what you're going to do. Let me know what you decide."

Emily reached out for Phillip's hand and squeezed it. She held his grey, stormy gaze and saw the emotion riding there. She'd hurt him. Perhaps he truly did love her. Perhaps she'd been too quick to judge him. "I'm sorry, Phillip. I really am."

For what? Loving someone else? It wasn't like she could help that, but her pregnancy added salt to an already open wound, and she hated that she'd hurt him. Better to hurt than to be hurt? Not so much as it turned out.

How much guilt had her father carried with him throughout his life? She'd never know. He'd disappeared without a backward glance, but now she knew he couldn't have walked away unscathed. Her father had to live with what he'd done. He'd made a choice. A choice he had to live with every day of his life. She hoped that burden was heavy. She hoped he missed her. She hoped he'd learned from his mistake.

Love was forever. Like a brand or a scar. It was jagged and sharp and pierced deeply enough to gouge the soul. She reached for the ring on the chain around her neck. "Thank you for asking me to marry you."

There was an ache in his grey gaze, and it pained her to see it. "I'm sure you will find the woman of your dreams. I'm sorry it isn't me."

"I'm sorry it isn't you, too, my dear."

"There's no need to reschedule the interview. I'm going to have this baby and I'm going to love her so much that she'll never have to question whether she's worthy of being loved. Whether she's beautiful enough or smart enough."

"You're worthy of being loved, Emily, but I'm not sure your farmer is." He took her hand and squeezed it.

"Thank you for caring." Emily smiled at Phillip through her tears. "Thank you for supporting me and loving me." She took a choppy breath, relieved to have told him the truth.

"I'm here if you need me."

There was warmth in his tone, but the rigidity in his jaw told her he was hurt. Hurt and angry. Hurt and disappointed. He dropped her hand and turned his gaze towards the water and the silvery path of the moon across the blackening waves.

She got the sense he'd already disengaged and turned his mind to moving on. There were more pretty fish in the sea. It wasn't like she didn't know it, but her emotions pitched and rolled, and maybe it was the pregnancy that made her so sentimental. She fought to control the hitch in her breath. "Thank you."

"Are you going to tell the farmer the truth?"

"I'm not sure he'll believe the baby's his." She'd been away more often than she'd been home. Would he trust her enough to believe it was his or would he demand a paternity test? And if he did, would she ever forgive him?

Emily sat until the glow of twilight was doused by darkness and the moon shimmered across the water. The stars shone and sparkled like broken glass or shattered dreams or unwanted diamonds.

She could be one of the top models in the world. More than half of the women on the Forbes list for The Highest Paid Models were VS Angels. With Phillip by her side? He was right. They'd be one hell of a force. That thought alone was tempting.

She hadn't planned on having a child. She'd been a parent since her earliest memories. Those wings were much more than a career goal. They represented freedom. Financial freedom. Freedom to soar. To be something. To be someone.

A pregnancy could be dealt with. It wasn't a child yet. It wasn't a baby yet. She had a choice. A choice every woman had the right to make.

An impossible choice. For her.

It would leave a scar way deeper and uglier than the one on Nick's face. The cost was too high. Her baby. Nick's baby. She rested her hand on her belly and comforted the small life inside.

The irony was bitter on her tongue.

She'd wear angel wings and boots of concrete. Every step on that catwalk would remind her of what she'd given up. She couldn't do it.

But what if the baby had Down syndrome? How would she cope with the guilt? Her father hadn't coped with it. Nor had her mother. She might carry that genetic propensity.

Having a baby was risky. Anything could go wrong. She'd be a single mother without an income. Her childhood flashed before her eyes until tears blurred the light of the moon. She was looking down the same cold, dark, barrel her mother had and now she realised how frightening it was. Worse. She would have to rely on Beverley and that was shaky ground.

Did she need to tell Nick? What if he demanded she get rid of it? Or was it her body, her baby, her decision? A part of her already loved that small spark of life. A part of her wanted that spark more than she'd wanted her father to stay. More than she'd wanted a perfect set of chromosomes for Carmie. More than she'd wanted the fancy feathers of her VS Angel wings.

How could she turn her back on the security of a guaranteed income? And a great income. An income that would secure their future. She had responsibilities. Her thoughts tangled and knotted and tangled some more. She couldn't indulge the fanciful delusions that danced before her, gilded by the light of the moon... a mini-Nick and a mini-Emily, who frolicked in the water, silver droplets shining on their wet skin, the sound of laughter. Her mum and sister relied on her. How had she let this happen?

Emily struggled to her feet and turned towards the hotel. Her career was the scaffolding that kept her strong. Without it?

She was Carmen Stone's knocked-up younger sister. Beverley Straun's wilful daughter who got what she deserved.

Chapter Ten

Nick stood on the Tankerton Jetty, the boards solid beneath his feet, the sea surging below. The ferry grew from a dot to a splash of colour to a fully-fledged vessel and Emily was there, on the deck, her eyes glued to his. His heart did a happy dance and banged so hard against the cage of his ribs, he had to press his hand to his chest. *Be still, my beating heart.* His stomach churned with every emotion from excitement to fear and everything in between. Elated. Exhilarated. Sick with rising worry… what if things had changed? What if she'd met someone else? What if her feelings towards him had cooled? What if Phillip had charmed her and she'd fallen for it? *Give her more credit*, he growled.

With mere metres between them, he waited, his breath still, his heart thumping. His grip tightened on the bottle of cold water he'd brought for her. The day was already hot and the sun-scorched boards of the pier burned through the soles of his loafers. The water heaved and breathed with a rhythmic pulse. Emily looked stiff, and he could tell from the moment she pushed off the rail and stood near the exit that she carried more than her Louis Vuitton suitcase. Something dragged her square shoulders forward. Something stole her smile. Something made her clutch her belly like she'd been sucker punched. And then he realised she was pale. Paler than pale. Green. Sick.

He lurched forward and leapt down the wooden steps to where the ramp was being lowered across to the pier. He stepped aside while an older man with a hiking pack pushed past and then he bounded onto the boat. She was curled over the side of the vessel, retching. He put his arm around her. She'd lost weight. What the hell was going on? She'd sounded fine on the phone. She wasn't fine.

When she straightened, he reached into his pocket for a handkerchief and handed it to her. She wiped her mouth and swiped at the tears. Her hair was pulled back into a ponytail and she looked like a dewy-eyed teenager, but what swirled in her eyes scared the bejesus out of him. "Geez, Stone. What can I do? Here. Drink." He handed over the bottle of cold water.

She guzzled it gratefully and when she was done, he pulled her into his arms and held her for the longest moment. Her dress had shoestring straps and the curve of her shoulder was velvety soft under his chin. She was here. They were together. Finally. He clung to the solid warmth of her, his nose nestled into the silky softness of her hair. The sun burned relentlessly from a cloudless sky and she wilted against him like the heat or the sickness had sapped her strength. The small moment was a big one marked by the metronomic slap of the waves against the side of the boat.

"I hope you're okay, miss."

The voice came from a distance. Nick pulled back and reached for Emily's suitcase. He needed to get her home. Carmie and Joey were past excited waiting for her to arrive and if Beverley hadn't intervened, Carmie would have been here beside him. He was quietly glad he'd gotten to pick Em up alone.

"When you're ready, miss, we need to get on our way. Sorry it's been such a tough crossing for you."

"Yes. Thank you. I'm fine." Her voice sounded drained.

"Some folks are prone to seasickness. You'll feel better once you're on dry land and it's real dry this time of year."

That was an understatement. It was tinder-dry, Nick thought. He helped Emily across the ramp, his arm around her, his other hand wrapped tightly around the leather handle of her suitcase. He'd rushed the feed-out that morning, the cows hungry for their haylage, and they'd already sought the shade of the trees, their tails swishing at the flies. It was hot. Damn hot. Beyond the boards of the pier, the land shimmered with heat. There wasn't a drop of rain forecast anytime soon.

Emily leaned against him and he wrapped his arm around her waist. Halfway along the pier, he stopped and studied her face. Her smile was rueful, mixed with happy-to-see-you and hell-I-feel-bad. She must have taken that ferry ride a hundred times and he'd never known her to be sick before. There were plenty of occasions when Western Port Bay hadn't played nice. "What's going on, Em. You don't get seasick. Is it food poisoning? A virus? Are you okay?"

She nodded. "It must be the heat." Her voice was fractured and cracked like his mother's old Royal Doulton china.

"There's plenty of that. You could fry an egg on the bonnet of the ute. The land's parched and only the snakes are happy about it. Don't suppose you brought some rain in that suitcase of yours. It feels heavy enough."

No laugh. Scarcely a smile. "I missed you." He wanted to kiss her. He wanted to drop the damn suitcase and hold her close. He wanted to ask her to marry him and never let her go… but he needed to get her home and out of the sun. Patience, man.

Patience.

"I missed you, too."

She looked pale and her skin shone with perspiration. "Stay here and I'll bring the car over." What was it about this woman and her shoes? The strappy high heels couldn't have been more impractical. Or more sexy. Holy cow. Her flowy summer dress looked stunning against her golden skin. He shifted his gaze to the ute and saw the shade had already moved beyond it. It would be hot in the cab. By the time he turned back, she was curled over, retching. Nick flung the suitcase in the back and leapt into the front seat of the vehicle. He floored it and with a sharp pull on the hand brake, skidded in the dust and stones. He leapt out before it stopped moving.

"Crikey, Stone. That's some heat stroke you've got going there. Here. Water."

She took a grateful sip and he helped her into the front passenger seat. He shot around to his own side and turned the air conditioning to full blast. She needed to cool down. He needed to cool down. Hell, his temperature spiked every time he looked at her. She must be the only woman in history who looked sexy whilst curled over barking her guts up.

"Get me home, Wheatley. Please."

"Oh, I plan to. I'm under strict instructions. No detours."

"I'm not up for detours." Her tone was brittle and washed-out.

He reached for her hand, which was clammy and limp. "Let me know if you need me to pull over." There was a very good chance of chuck in his vehicle and he pressed his foot to the metal, but the banging of the corrugations and Emily's groan had him slowing down.

"Stop the car!"

He pulled over with a spray of stones and Emily leapt out to throw up again. He got out and crouched beside her, waiting until she was done. He wrapped his arm around her. "You must have a tummy bug."

Emily collapsed against him like a rag doll, her eyes filling with tears. Her body shook. She'd definitely lost weight. She felt slight and bony. Something was wrong. Fear roared in his ears. "What is it, Stone. What's going on?"

She took a breath, the narrow frame of her shoulder digging into his ribs and stared out to the horizon, her eyes glazed.

"It's less of a tummy bug, Wheatley. And more of a baby. I'm pregnant."

"Oh." Her words, weak and quiet, near knocked him flat. Like being hit by a Massey Ferguson or ten. Air pushed from his lungs and his knees buckled.

"You're going to be a daddy, if I survive this morning sickness, which for the record, lasts most of the day. You're a virulent man." She gazed at him with sadness in her eyes. Despair. Strength.

He couldn't move. He couldn't get his words together. He didn't know whether to laugh and holler or grovel and apologise. He gasped for air like his lungs had collapsed and oxygen was in short supply.

"*I* did this to you?" He'd made her sick? Pregnant? "Are you sure?"

Her eyes darkened like a cloud had blocked the sun and she sagged against him. "I'm sure, but I understand if you want a paternity test done."

"Stone, I meant are you sure you're pregnant. Not are you sure it's mine." It hadn't even occurred to him that it might not be, but now that she'd planted the seed, the thought curled inside him like a venomous snake. Phillip? Was that cad still in the picture? Someone else? Jealousy blinded him and his vision turned the colour of blood. No. Phillip wasn't a contender. Nick forced air into his constricted lungs. He knew that. He knew it from the tips of his toes to the end of his nose. And he knew Emily. She was strong. Fierce in the best kind of way. She wasn't easily wooed. His vision cleared and his attention shifted from himself to the beautiful woman who carried his child.

"It's definitely yours." She tried to smile, but emotions stormed in her eyes like a winter blast through the manna and swamp gums. "The question is, Wheatley, was this your plan all along? Get me pregnant so I'm forced to stay?"

Her light-hearted tone clashed with the brevity in her eyes. "No. Hell, no. You think I did this on purpose?" Anger razed inside him, hotter than the damn sun which near burned the skin off his bones. "To *force* you to come back to me?" He got to his feet and his temper wound tight like a category five cyclonic wind. "You think me capable of that?" Of course, she did.

He strode across to the barbed wire fence that demarcated the farmland from the road and stared across the bleached landscape and the parched earth towards The Pinnacles, which rose high and hazy in the heat. His thoughts raced like flame across the tinder-dry terrain. How could she think he'd done this on purpose to trap her? Because she was Charliese's best friend and she knew he was capable of awful things. He might not have driven her off the road and drowned her, but he'd ruined her life just the same. There was no hiding with Emily. And whilst he might not have done this on purpose, she was pregnant, and he was the father.

A part of him was elated. A part of him wanted this child more than he wanted rain.

But not like this.

This changed everything. Before they got started. Before they got off the ground. Her dreams and goals and plans didn't include breastfeeding and nappies and pureed food. It wasn't like she could leave a child and head overseas for weeks at a time. Some women might and he wasn't one to judge, but Emily wouldn't. He knew that without asking.

He'd wanted her to come home when the time was right. Not because she was knocked up and had no choice.

He'd wanted her to marry him because she loved him, not because she was pregnant, and he was to blame. She'd end up resenting him. She already resented him. His heart sank like he'd leapt from the top of The Pinnacles.

He turned back to where she sat, pale and limp. His chest hurt like she'd taken his heart in her fist and squeezed. He'd done this to her. He'd brought her to this. Kneeling in the dirt. Her life ruined.

"I'm sorry, Stone. I'm sorry you have to deal with this. I'm sorry you feel terrible." Any love she felt for him would be gone. Purged into the dry earth. How could she ever forgive him? His nostrils flared and he grabbed at the scalding air like a man gasping his final breath.

"I'm sorry, too, Wheatley. I know you didn't do this on purpose." She sat back on her heels, her glamorous dress in the red dust and dry grass, her eyes bleak. "I had to say no to my dream job with Victoria's Secret and I feel like crap. I look like crap. I smell like crap... well, puke. I'm sorry I doubted you. This was my fault as much as yours."

Nick battled the rampaging emotions that thundered inside

of him. "You were offered a job with Victoria's Secret?" His two-dollar-shop angel wings now seemed cruel. He'd wanted to gift her something special. He'd shattered her dream. He'd ruined her life. He'd left her with a synthetic substitute that couldn't come close to the real thing. He tasted bile, bitter and acerbic. "The timing isn't good. But you have a choice and I'll support you in whatever you decide. I know how important your career is to you and how much you want to be a Victoria's Secret Angel."

It was like swallowing blades. He wanted to demand that she keep the baby. He wanted to rush to protect it. He wanted their child. He wanted it more than a perfect face. He wanted it more than his next breath. But this was Emily's dream. His mouth turned dry—drier than the cracked earth—and tasted of the dust that swirled in the air, gritty and bitter. The decision wasn't his to make. Emily had the most to lose and he had the most to gain. He would support her, whatever she decided.

What if she chose to terminate the pregnancy? The thought alone was enough to drown him. Another child. Another death. A sibling for the one who haunted him.

A car flashed past in the periphery of his vision and his lungs filled with choking dust. His chest near exploded.

"Marry me, Stone." The words were out before he'd had time to think. Foolish, deluded man. Like she'd want to marry him when she'd thought for even a moment, he was capable of trapping her with an unwanted pregnancy. "I'm in this for the long haul, no matter what." His pride was the least of his worries.

A battle raged in her eyes. In the flicker of her frown. In the stiffness of her shoulders. "I can't, Wheatley. But thanks for the offer."

And true to form, she pushed him away. Well, he wasn't so easily pushed.

He tried not to think of Carmie and their surprise proposal. He was a complete and utter fool, and Emily was pregnant with his child. Every instinct told him to retreat. But Emily was hurting. She was sick. She was confused. And he'd done this to her. One way or another.

"It's going to be okay. We'll work this out together." His stomach contracted. He didn't need to think. He wanted this child. He wanted a family with her. But his needs were not the most important consideration here. She had to feel ready and he knew how much of a struggle that would be.

And then it occurred to him. She was here. Pregnant. Offering him a say in the matter. If she'd wanted to terminate the pregnancy, she was more than capable of quietly managing the problem. "You're planning to keep it, aren't you? You want this child as much as I do." Oxygen rushed into his lungs.

Maybe she loved him after all.

But maybe she didn't trust him to love her back.

"*We* can do this, Em. We can do this together." The tightness around his chest eased and he heard a gull screech overhead, like the world had held its breath, silent and still, but now moved and returned to vivid colour and sound. "I've delivered calves you know. I know what I'm doing."

"Are you saying we won't get to a hospital on time because we live in the back of nowhere? That's not what I was afraid of… or at least it wasn't. Having a baby is risky."

"You're not your mum, Em, and I'm not your dad."

"What if I am like my mum? What if you are like my dad and we just haven't been tested yet? I didn't plan on having children. Ever." She glared at him, her dark eyes like grenades.

"What if our baby has Carmie's chromosomal abnormality? What then?"

"I love Carmie's chromosome abnormality. We can work this out. We can be brave together."

"What if you decide to go back to Hollywood to direct those movies you've been writing?" Emily lashed out at him with panic in her eyes. "What if you go back to being the man you were?"

"You're creating obstacles, Stone, because you're too freaking scared to believe someone might love you enough to stay when the going gets tough." He held her chocolate gaze, his tone solid. A rock in the wild seas that bucketed in her eyes. "It was Phillip who helped me realise I'm not the man I was. That man would have been impressed by him and I promise you, I wasn't. It was you who helped me realise how happy I am here. And Carmie. I've got nothing to prove. This place has brought me more happiness and joy than acting and fame ever did."

Emily wanted to believe him. A part of her feared the man she loved wasn't real, but his eyes burned like blue flame and tenderness softened the planes of his face, his crooked, imperfect, adorable face. Her heart swelled and filled her chest. Energy rushed through her body and for a long moment, she allowed herself to think it might work out.

But then she realised what he'd said… she was too scared to believe he *might* love her. He'd said marry me. Like it was a solution to the problem.

He's the kind of man who does the right thing. It's a pity proposal. He doesn't love you.

Maybe he was right. She was too damn scared to trust him. She armoured herself against every voice in her head. She didn't trust him to love her. Love didn't feel safe. The only person she could rely on was herself. "I need my career. I'm responsible for my family's well-being." Fresh tears welled in her eyes.

"How are you going to work with a newborn?"

"I don't know, but I can't expect you to support us all."

"Yes, you can. I promised I'd watch over your people. But if you need to work to feel safe, then you'll work. And if you need to travel to escape, then you'll travel. And we'll be here when you're ready to come home. I'm not going anywhere."

Her reasons sounded childish when he put them like that, but they were real, and he hadn't discounted them. He hadn't tried to fix her or change her or take away her safety net. Perhaps those were the words she'd needed to hear. She wouldn't have believed a declaration of love anyway. He'd promised he would be there for her... for their child. For her family. And he stood beside her like Dr. Seuss's south-going Zax facing her north-going Zax, stubborn and unmoving.

Her head cleared. Her body stopped churning. Her lungs filled with air. She could do this. It would be okay. "You're not the only one with scars, Wheatley."

"I know it."

"I come with my sister. My mum. My hang-ups."

"I know it and I love them all." He lifted her hand to his lips and kissed her palm, the soft brush of his lips draining her more than the heat and the sickness.

"Even my hang-ups?"

He turned her hand and kissed each knuckle as he spoke. "Every... single... one... of... them. The pretty bits and the not-so-pretty bits."

"What if I'm not the woman you think I am?" A silent plea

rang in her ears. *Don't love me. Don't believe in me.*

"You're more, way more, than you believe, Stone. And you're more, way more, than I deserve."

He reached for his handkerchief and wiped the wetness from her cheek. The blue fire of his gaze consumed her, and she wanted him, her body stirring and aching and clenching, her pulse thrumming, her cells vibrating with the same tension she saw in the set of his stubbled jaw.

"I like my job. It helps me feel seen. I don't want to feel invisible."

"You'll never be invisible to me."

He wiped the wisps of hair back from her face and his touch, designed to comfort, did the exact opposite. It stirred sensations she didn't want to feel. Sensations that left her weak and wanting. He lowered his mouth to hers and the firm press of his lips swept her away, the unbearable ache of missing him melting into a different kind of ache. He pulled her close and held her. She wrapped her arms around the solid strength of him, her cheek against the smooth cotton of his shirt and the heated muscle that curved beneath. She felt the steady thrum of his heart and savoured the warm salty scent of him—a musky, outdoorsy, male scent that said, Nick or home. Her heart thudded in time with his and she wanted… she wanted all that she feared.

"We need to get you home."

Nick stepped back, inviting distance between them and Emily felt like her flesh had been torn. A part of her wanted to hold him forever and never let go. She forced her hands back to her side and focused on the sharp jab of the stones under the soles of her sandals.

His gaze said he cared, and his kindness was harder to

manage than his anger.

"And that attention you seek, Stone? That adoration you enjoy?" His gaze bored into hers. "It's not real. Where will it be in twenty years? In ten years? Don't delude yourself. It's a dog-eat-dog world you live in. Those people feed off you. Phillip loves the way you make him look. How powerful you make him feel."

"You don't miss Hollywood?"

"No. Being a celebrity didn't make me happy. It made me arrogant. It made me less. I don't miss it, but if that's what you want, you're welcome to it. I won't stop you." He reached for her hands. "I'm here because I want to be here. My home is here. My heart is here."

My heart is yours.

The words sounded in her head, even though he didn't say them. He stroked her hands and her muscles loosened. Tears ran down her cheek and she sobbed, her breath catching in her throat. A breeze stirred the dry grass beyond the barbed wire fence, giving it life. Cattle stood in silent groups under the shade of the trees, their tails swishing from side to side. There was the sound of blow flies. The hum of bees. The distant wash of water against the rocky shore. He couldn't have known, but his words were the right ones.

Emily squeezed his hands and held on like he might float off into the sky. "I'm glad. I like farmer-Nick."

"I'm relieved to hear it. Now, let's get you out of the heat. I don't need to wonder what kind of a mother you'll make for our child. I already know. I already love that person. Carmie loves that person. The rest is bullshit. I see it as clear as the sky above us. Don't fall for the fairy dust, Stone."

Nick settled Emily in the car and stared across the brown landscape to the glistening blue of the sea. The trees by the roadside were covered with a layer of dust. Everything looked parched and bleached and burned. He closed the door and strode around to the driver's side. A lizard scuttled away in the undergrowth and the sun seared through his best shirt. Today was supposed to be perfect. Instead, the timing of their little surprise was all wrong.

Nick revved the engine. "I'm sorry you've had to deal with this alone. I'm sorry you're sick, but my decision is easy. There's nothing in the world I want more than to have a family with you. This changes nothing. I love you. The real you. I love the woman who held a calf's head out of the water and near froze to death so it wouldn't drown. I love the woman who taught her sister to play snakes and ladders like a pro. I love the woman who makes a house a home just by walking into a room. I want a family with you. I want a life with you, Stone. I want a home with you."

"What if something goes wrong, Wheatley? What then?"

"Then we'll deal with it. I adore Carmie. If we have a child with Down syndrome, I'll adore him or her, too. I don't care what people think of me. Not anymore. I don't care how I look to others. I have you to thank for that. And Carmie. Your sister is a joy. Why would you worry about that?"

"Because I always wished she was perfect."

"You wished she was perfect because you blamed her disability for scaring your father away. It wasn't Carmie's fault. It was your father's fault for believing other people's opinions were more important than the love he felt for his own family. A marriage is between two people. Maybe his relationship with your mum made him feel less. Maybe it had nothing to do with either one of you."

"I don't want to love you."

"I know it, but I'm glad that you do. And I'm guessing that despite everything you still love your dad. You have a lot of love to give."

"He left us. He never looked back." Tears pooled in her eyes and he took her hands in his.

"Maybe he was too ashamed of his own weakness." Now that was a feeling he could relate to. He tried not to think of Charliese, and her baby buried deep in the hot, parched earth.

"Maybe."

"Maybe he believed he'd failed you and couldn't face you. He did fail you. But that doesn't mean I'll fail you."

You failed Charliese.

He heard the words even though she didn't say them. You failed her child. What if you fail our child? "I can't change the past, Stone. I can only promise you that I will love and protect you until my dying breath."

"Out of a sense of duty because I'm pregnant with your child." Her breath hitched and a tear rolled down her cheek.

"I love you, Stone. I love who you are. I love the woman behind the makeup and the designer clothes. Of course, I have a sense of duty. I'm responsible. You didn't get pregnant alone." He directed the air conditioning blast towards her, and the car motor idled with a soothing hum.

"I love this baby. I love it more than I thought I could. Even though it makes me sick." Emily wrapped her arms around her stomach as if to hold it close. Colour returned to her cheeks and the rigidity in her spine softened. "I couldn't have..." She took a deep breath and held his gaze. His insides near ignited. He couldn't have wanted her more. "You had a right to a choice, too, Wheatley. I'm glad you chose us."

She'd wanted to give him an out. She'd tried to convince him this wasn't a viable option, when it was perfect from every angle. He had no doubt she could cope alone and manage it all, but she didn't have to.

Frustration tangled his insides into knots. What did he have to say to convince her he loved her?

"I'm glad you chose to keep our baby, Stone." His child. He eyed her flat stomach, her slender figure, and a blast of protectiveness near stole his breath. Never would he let her down. Never would he forget how blessed he was to have her in his life. How he adored her. How special he wanted her life to be, every day. He took her hands in his and the dull, life-weary glaze that had haunted her eyes cleared. She smiled and he was like a fool moth who couldn't resist the light. "I want to marry you, right here, right now. Let's find a pastor."

"We're on French Island. We live in the back of nowhere. And I haven't agreed to marry you." The light in her eyes faded and his heartbeat slowed. It slowed until his body was silent. Until he could have heard a leaf fall from a tree anywhere on the island. Her gaze skittered to the view over his shoulder. "Phillip proposed to me."

His muscles bunched and his brow beaded with sweat. The small moment of silence stretched all the way to the horizon. He dropped her hands like he'd picked up a spiky toadfish by mistake. That smiling bastard. She'd fallen for his act. He knew a good actor when he saw one, and that guy deserved an Oscar. Phillip didn't love Emily—he was too in love with himself. He didn't deserve her. Nick struggled to draw breath into his chest. It was like Charliese had reached out of the water and pulled him under. "Tell me you're not going to marry him." Not the grinning assassin.

Emily looked confused, like he'd spun her around blind-folded. "Why would I marry Phillip?"

Nick cupped his hands around her face and looked her straight in the eyes. "I love you. Please marry me and make us a family. You are the only woman I love. Only you. You and this baby—our baby—"

"I'm not going to say yes when your hand has been forced. You need time to digest all of this. You might change your mind."

"I've had weeks to think about marrying you—I missed you more than I can say—and your pregnancy is the best news ever." He sealed it with a kiss. A long, slow paralysing kiss. "There is nothing I'd like more than to marry you and have a child with you."

He planted his lips on hers with no apology and her fragile smile near fried him to a crisp. "Let's go. I have something to show you."

Chapter Eleven

N ick pulled up in front of While Away and Emily couldn't believe what she saw. Pink balloons. Everywhere. Tied to the gate. Weighed down and lined up alongside the driveway. And a sign on the gate in Carmie's writing that read: Welcome Home. Her eyes welled with tears. Again. "Wow."

"We all wanted you to know how much you were missed."

"It looks amazing. The garden looks amazing."

"Carmie and I planted camellias. Lots of them. And I put in a bore, so they'll never go thirsty. Nor will the grass, which will keep Carmie's mate, Joey, happy."

"You did this for Carmie? I can't thank you enough."

"Carmie loves camellias."

"I know. *She'll* want to marry you. She'll never forgive me if I become your wife."

"She wants *you* to marry me. Take a closer look at the driveway."

Emily stepped out of the vehicle and reeled as a wave of heat hit her like a tsunami. It stole her breath, leaving her light-headed. She forced the hot air into her lungs and stepped forward. The driveway was covered in flowers. Flowers carefully arranged to form letters. *Marry Me, Love Nick. Marry*

Him, Love Carmie. And a big heart.

Nick took her by the shoulders and turned her towards him. She couldn't see him for tears, couldn't speak, she was so choked up with happiness. "You were going to ask me to marry you? Before you found out I was pregnant?"

"I was." Nick reached into his pocket and pulled out a ring. Bought from a two-dollar shop. A pink flower on a silver-plated band. Carefully chosen by Carmie because they had to get this right. She didn't want Em to say no and the only person who loved camellias more than Carmie was Em. He hadn't known that about her, but Carmie had. They'd been his mother's favourite flower, too, and everything had clicked into place for him. She was the woman of his dreams. The woman who'd banished his nightmares.

"I love it. How did you know I love pink camellias?"

"Carmie and I got talking."

"I can see that. Hey, they can't be real. Not at this time of year."

"They're silk. What do you think? Will you marry me? Please? You haven't answered yet." He didn't want to beg, but he would. He dropped to his knee—the cheap bauble held out like the finest of gems.

"How can I say no when you asked so perfectly?"

Her eyes dropped to the ring and she smiled a smile he hadn't seen before, but it was his favourite by far. Blinding, yes. Glowing, always. But her lip quivered ever so slightly, and the smile shone from her eyes like a full moon over the ocean. Soft. Silvery. Seductive. She took his breath away.

"Yes, Wheatley. I'll marry you."

He leapt to his feet and drew her into his arms, pressing his lips against hers. "It's what you want? I haven't worn you down?"

"It's everything I want. You're everything I want."

"You're everything *I* want." He took the kiss deeper and she melted into his arms. He lost track of where she finished, and he began.

"Nick! Em!" Carmie's voice came from the distance. He pulled back and gazed into Emily's eyes. What he saw reflected there filled him with hope. He leaned close and spoke into her ear. "We're having a baby. We're going to be married. We're going to be a family. I couldn't be happier."

Emily swallowed the fear that rose in her throat like a sea snake, but her answer was as clear as the vast blue sky above. "Yes."

Nick reached for her hand and slipped the oversized, sparkly, glitzy piece of costume-bling on to her left ring finger. "I thought you'd like to choose your own ring. We can swap this for the real thing when you're ready. We could have one made and incorporate the diamond from Charliese's ring if you like. Or not. I know how special she was to you. And I love her for bringing you to me."

"She was." For the longest moment, Emily gazed into the fathomless blue of his eyes. What stirred in her heart was as enduring as the universe, as solid as the earth, as free as the air. She couldn't move. Couldn't break the magic until Carmie and Joey were upon them. Carmie wore pink angel wings on her back and a smile that near blinded. Emily pulled away and wrapped her arms around her sister. "Shall we tell Carmie the good news?"

"Did she say yes, Nick?" Carmie asked, her eyes bright, her chest heaving.

"Sure did, sweet cheeks."

"Yes!" Carmie jumped with excitement, her fist in the air.

"And guess what?" Emily waited until Carmie's gaze turned upwards.

"What?"

"You're going to be an auntie. We're having a baby."

"Did you hear that, Nick? I'm going to be an auntie."

Nick grinned and Emily felt it all the way to her toes. Gone was the heavy feeling that had dragged at her for days. They were going to be a family.

"Is it my turn, now?" Carmie couldn't stay still. She was revved to the max. "Nick, is it my turn?"

"Sure is," he said with a wink in Emily's direction. "Carmie, will you be my friend, my sister-in-law, and my buddy for always?"

"Yes, Nick. Yes. Do I get a ring, too?"

"Sure do." Nick pulled out a ring identical to the one Emily could feel, cool against her left ring finger. Her heart hitched and tears rolled from her eyes. Her sister looked so happy, so bursting with joy. Her exhilaration increased a thousand-fold if that was even possible.

"Stay still for half a second," Nick admonished.

Carmie couldn't. She danced around and screamed and ya-hooed, and Emily couldn't stop the smile or the overwhelming love when her sister hugged her around the stomach and near crushed the life out of the poor baby nestled there. Thank goodness it was tiny and resilient.

Nick went down on his knee and carefully put the ring on Carmie's finger.

"Look, Em. I got a ring, too. Nick's going to be my brother. Yes!" She punched her fist into the air and hollered for Joey to come and take a look at her ring. He was distracted by the

182

grass. Green grass, watered from the bore. Their home was like an oasis in the dry Australian bush.

Emily turned and saw her mum standing on the veranda. She kissed Nick, a deep, loving connection. "I couldn't love you more." She pulled away and rushed towards her mum, careful not to step on the perfectly placed flowers. She wanted a photo so she could remember this forever.

"Hi, Mum. You're up. You look so much better. There's colour in your cheeks." Her mum had put on weight. Gone was the grey tinge. The lanky hair. She even had lipstick on.

"Congratulations, beautiful girl. You have a beautiful man there."

"I sure do." Emily hugged her mum and whispered for her ears only. "You're going to be a grandma in six months."

Her mum pushed her back and stared at her with wide eyes, her expression overjoyed. "You're pregnant?"

"Yes. And it wasn't planned, which was probably just as well because I don't think I ever would have been ready to take that leap of faith."

"That's the best news. I'm thrilled. I can't wait. This day just keeps getting better and better."

"I love you, Mum."

"I love you, too, sweetie. So much." Her mum stepped off the veranda and Emily saw Nick behind her with a sexy, lopsided grin. Her heart shifted in her chest and she reached for the small life that nestled in her womb. Her family. Her special people. Never had she felt so blessed. So grateful.

Her mum wrapped Nick in a hug. "Welcome to the family, Nick. Again. For always. I'm thrilled to be a grandma. I can't wait."

"Thanks, Bev." He had his arm around Carmie, and Em could

smell cinnamon, sweet and spicy. Suddenly, she was hungry. Past hungry. Famished.

"Is that apple pie I smell?"

"It sure is. Nick and I made the pastry." Carmie dragged her by the hand and together they walked into the kitchen. Nick joined them and Carmie danced and hollered. "Nick, do I get a ring for being an auntie? Can I get a purple one this time? Then I'll have two."

"You bet." Nick wrapped his arm around Emily. She leaned into his solid, muscular bulk and all of the stress of the last few weeks melted away. This was home and home was the only place she wanted to be.

"Yay!" Carmie shrieked, her voice excited and happy. "Joey, look at my ring."

"Hey, can I get a purple one, too? When the baby's born?" Emily turned towards the man who had taken her world and coloured it with pink. Her favourite colour. He pressed his lips against hers and her heart soared.

"You can have whatever ring you want. We got you wings, too. White ones. Because you're my kind of angel."

He'd thought of everything. "How about a single band of gold?"

"Sounds perfect." He grinned and her heart squeezed in her chest.

"This is going to work."

"Damn right it is. We're going to make it work. *You* are where I want to be. You are my happy place. You are my special person, more important to me than anything or anyone."

"More important than apple pie and ice cream?"

Nick pretended to ponder, and she laughed.

"Yes!" called Carmie. "The pie's ready. I love my ring. Thanks

184

Nick. Em, do you love yours? I helped Nick choose it."

"Yes, more than anything. You've both been very busy." She moved to get the pie out of the oven, but her mum was one step ahead of her.

"I've got it, love. You sit down and let me take care of you."

Emily grinned. So that's all it took. She should have gotten knocked up years ago. "Thanks, Mum." She lowered herself into a chair and admired her ring. "Great choice, Carmie and Nick. I love it." She felt like the luckiest girl alive. She was loved by a man who saw the imperfect woman behind the perfect face and loved her anyway. Better still, she loved him with all of her heart. They were so much more together than she was alone. With Nick, she'd found something real. A love like her grandparents' and a life on the land they'd cherished. It was a connection that grounded her. A connection that eased the flighty sensation that scooted inside her when she hoped and wanted and couldn't have. Here was peace and happiness and freedom. Here was everything she'd longed for and everyone she loved.

She was home. And Nick's love for her—her love for him—gave her the only kind of wings she needed. Wings that lifted her soul. Wings that healed her heart.

* * *

Thank you so much for reading Shatterproof! I hope you enjoyed Emily and Nick's story. I really enjoyed writing it and this one is close to my heart given my day job as a child psychologist.

I read about 'glass' children a while ago, and I see a lot of kids with special needs through my work at the hospital. I really wanted to give their siblings a voice through the characters in this series. The siblings of a special needs child can feel like their own needs are less important. Some 'glass children', like the heroine in Shatterproof, step in to care for their sibling and parent/s (see the TED presentation by Alicia Arenas, Recognising Glass Children: www.youtube.com/watch?v=MSwqo-g2Tbk).

If you were a 'glass' child—or carry wounds from your childhood, which many of us do—I wish you love, compassion and kindness towards self. And healing.

Growing up, we had a farm at Corinella, across the bay from French Island. We loved to take our boat across and explore the island. On more than one occasion, the boat motor broke down before we got there and we had to row to shore or get rescued. While I was writing the story, Mr G and I took our kids to French Island by ferry from Stony Point and hired bikes at the general store. We pedalled along Mosquito Creek Road and spied koalas in the trees!

If you enjoyed *Shatterproof,* I'd very much appreciate a short review on your Amazon website of choice and/or on Goodreads: https://www.goodreads.com/book/show/52961990-shatterproof. Authors rely on readers' reviews to stand out (hopefully in a good way)!

I'd love to hear from you!

You can find me at www.lexigreene.com.au or on facebook at www.facebook.com/lexi.greene.75 or www.facebook.com/lovelexigreene or via email at lexigreene@aapt.net.au.

Sending love and hugs, and warmest regards,

Lexi Greene xx

About the Author

Lexi is an Australian author who loves to write powerful, passionate and provocative stories. She writes romance in the early morning and works as a paediatric neuropsychologist by day. A happily married mum of two teens, a parrot and a puppy, she loves to escape into a good story. She is a firm believer that a bath, a green tea, and chocolate take a good book and make it perfect.

Lexi is a member of Romance Writers of Australia and Romance Writers of America; and is a huge fan of Margie Lawson's Writer's Academy.

Lexi loves a happily ever after…

Also by Lexi Greene

Once Upon a Christmas Wish
Jenn Adams is determined to tick off her bucket list and face her past nemeses—learning to ski and a man named Brad.

Brad Oregon is the only man she's ever loved. His chocolate eyes. His to-die-for smile. His toned body. His very toned body.

But Brad's reputation with women is almost as renowned as his ski-racing success. Now a ski instructor in beautiful Whistler, he's as difficult to resist as the scenery! What the hell. Life is short. A two week holiday romance should suit them both perfectly. Right?

https://bklnk.com/B07LBM48NN

Bachelor on Trial

When Tony Radcliff joins Forbes lawyers, career-driven Scarlet O'Connor finds she has competition for the coveted partnership position.

And Tony has a couple of aces up his sleeve. Like his surf-sculpted body, which plays havoc with Scarlet's 'all work and no play' plans for partnership. And his brother, who holds the key to a secret from her past.

When Scarlet and Tony start steaming up the office windows, there's no doubt they're playing with fire. But there can only be one winner, so who gets burned?

https://bklnk.com/B08KPFWW7D

Desert Prince, Scandalous Affair

There is nothing Zahidah's Prince Rashid bin Ra'ed Al Shahid won't do to safeguard his family's honour and his kingdom's future.

And there is nothing Jemma Mason won't do to protect her daughter, Sami, the result of a crazy one-night connection with a dark, handsome cliché in a Sydney bar.

When Sami needs a bone marrow transplant to save her life, Jemma must travel to Zahidah and face the prince who has no idea he's a father. But when Princess Aminah, Rashid's sister, steps in and saves Sami's life (and Jemma's secret), there is nothing Jemma won't do for Aminah including rescuing her from an arranged marriage she dreads.

When Aminah is abducted, Prince Rashid wants answers and his questions lead him to Jemma and her web of lies.

Jemma can't resist Rashid's scandalous proposal but can he forgive her when he discovers the truth?

https://bklnk.com/B07G1RN2WR

Bachelor on Board

Success is the best revenge.

Amber Reed, a rising television producer, needs her new show—Bachelor on Board, Australia—to outshine the one her ex stole from her, or risk losing her job to the conniving Lothario, but when her Bachelor falls in love and absconds with one of the contestants, she's forced to rely on Plan B, Nathan Moretti, the high school popular who broke her heart.

Nathan Moretti, soon-to-be head of the wealthy Moretti family, needs a wife to protect the family fortune from his gold-digger stepmother, and his job should be easy with twenty-four beautiful women to choose from. Right?

Not when the only woman he wants is the one behind the camera and her success relies on him finding love with someone else, on screen, on schedule, as promised. Can Amber forgive the past and risk her heart—again?

https://bklnk.com/B08KPFWW7D